A Crumbling

ROSE

Steven with lots of love!

Linda Hughes

Linda Hughes

Books by Linda Hughes

Cloistered Secrets

Secrets Without Compromise

Yesterday Forever Gone

Possession of Willowland Manor

Justice for Jennifer

Best Seller Obsession

A Crumbling Rose

Visit Website: Linda L Hughes.com

Dedication

Penny

You came into our lives when we were dealing with the loss of our second Westie, Maggie. Since we'd had Maggie for sixteen years, we didn't think it could ever be possible to love another dog. However, since you were both sick and physically abused, we were unable to turn you away.

As time passed and you became confident that we wouldn't harm you, you have now flourished into a healthy and happy part of our family. Although you haven't wanted to sleep under my desk while I write—as Maggie did— you are now staying close by . . . except at mealtimes.

A Crumbling Rose

Chapter 1

(Present Day)

It seemed like she'd been traveling for a week, but in reality . . . Kendra had been on the road for a mere three days. Following the therapist's suggestions, she'd let go of planning every moment of every day, embarking on the trip to Texas without a single hotel reservation.

Since leaving California, the further eastward she ventured, the freeways changed from what seemed like ants following a trail to their food source to moving—mile upon mile—at a boring pace. At first, her favorite music helped to curtail the monotony, but eventually it too became repetitive . . . even tiresome.

Within sixty miles of her destination, the stark surroundings were apparent in everything she noticed. Closer yet to the target point, the hard and bumpy dirt roads were in such disrepair that she thought the car might vibrate apart. The few and far between structures were mostly dilapidated barns, but the most obvious change . . . the lack of a single passing vehicle.

The car's navigation system had quit working miles ago, and the telephone reception was spotty at best. Apprehensive that she might be going in the wrong direction, Kendra finally stopped to take a closer look at the spread-out map on the passenger seat. After turning off the car, Kendra momentarily panicked, wondering what she'd do if the car didn't start again. Then wondered . . . what if she needed help or died out there and no one could find her? Not only that, but since her mother's death, there was no one left who'd care . . . if indeed, her mother ever did.

Relieved and without difficulty, the car started. Even so, perhaps this trip wasn't the best idea after all. Maybe it would have been better to fly to San Antonio, rent a car, and ask her mother's attorney in Sabinal, Texas to take her to see the house. Oh well, too late now.

Kendra found Texas a lot different from what she was accustomed to in California . . . especially Los Angeles and the surrounding cities. Not only was the scenery different, but the people in Texas seemed more personable and down-to-earth. She found their direct way of communicating unique and sometimes amusing. At her last restaurant stop, the waitress said, "Howdy ma'am. If you're hungry and fixin' to eat, you picked the right spot." When Kendra nodded in the affirmative, the waitress followed with, "Well, sit yourself anywhere, but I'd stay clear of the little one pitchin' a hissy fit over yonder. His momma won't let him have a second piece of pie. Honey, I'll fetch a menu for y'all and be back directly."

Returning from her thoughts and wanting to give extra attention to the road ahead—knowing she had to be almost there—Kendra noticed cattle grazing on the rolling pastures on the right side, while the other side was a continual dense wooded area. The bronze glow of the afternoon sun seemed to settle on the passing pastures while the tree-lined side seemed dark and uninviting.

After running out of viable excuses during the last six months, Kendra grew tired of the lawyer in Sabinal hassling her to pick up the keys to her mother's house. She finally told him to mail the keys and include a map on the best way to get there. When she kept insisting, he bluntly answered, "You people in California don't make no sense . . . good sense, that is." He didn't give her a chance to comment on what she felt was a rude remark. After all, she was from California, and she used good sense . . . well, not often but sometimes . . . well, never according to her therapist. Perhaps the therapist was right but his remark was still rude.

Continuing on, he'd quickly added, "I haven't been to the house in quite some time . . . maybe it's been a year or two. There were some things stored in the attic that your momma didn't want any eyes but yours to see and not until after her death. I can't rightly say what she was talkin' 'bout or if anything is still there. That's for you to discover and sort out." Again, she told herself to quit thinking about the past, the attorney, her therapist, or anything else and just focus on finding the house.

Knowing she had to be close—Kendra almost passed the weathered sign leaning at a forty-five degree angle with faded letters: "THE OLD ROAD." Turning onto another dirt road—smaller but with numerous deep potholes—she smirked before saying out loud, "This road should be called: "THE WORSE ROAD YET." Frowning, she wished the road wasn't turning into the wooded side . . . making the road especially difficult to see and tricky to follow.

Watching the odometer, she needed to stay on this awful road for about half a mile. Finding the next turn—an opening but more like a trail between over-grown bushes— she hoped it would finally lead her to the house. This opening was the last written information on the attorney's small map. Slowly approaching the small gap, she feared the car was too wide to fit through it. Oh well, she'd come too far to quit now.

Listening to the scraping sounds against both sides of the car, steering proved to be both difficult and scary. At long last, a clearing appeared in front of a small house that was most likely white in color at one time. Some of the house was obscured by a massive tree, partially dead on the side nearest the house.

Feeling insecure, she again thought about being alone in no-where land and something terrible happening. Before stepping out of the car, she tried her phone again . . . still no signal. Why hadn't she told someone, even her therapist, about her plans to find her mother's house in Texas?

This time, she'd made a major senseless—even stupid—spur-of-the-moment decision. Chastising herself . . . this trip could be added to a long list of other bad choices she's made in the past. On second thought and if she survived this ordeal; her therapist might be proud of her for making a decision—even if a bad one—without it consuming her every moment. After fixating on the good, the bad, and the ugly memories during the drive, she needed to concentrate on the present and get with the program. After all, she'd finally gotten to the house. Sighing, Kendra removed the two keys from her pants pocket . . . one for the house and one for the attic.

Pausing a moment in front of the house, Kendra took a closer look at the half-dead tree. The previously considered dead part was actually a huge dried branch that had broken off and fallen against the house, crushing the end section of the front porch and the connecting railings.

Doing her best to maneuver around large cracks and broken boards, she managed to climb up the porch steps leading to the front door. Thoughts continued to rush through her head like: what would she find inside? Would the attic be full of interesting memorabilia? Worse case scenario, would she find both the house and attic completely empty?

Grasping the dirty door knob, Kendra inserted and twisted the larger of the two keys. After a slight hesitation and a hard push inward, the door opened. Her immediate reaction had nothing to do with what she first saw or didn't see but more about the pungent stench and oppressive stale air that smacked her in the face.

Having speculated for months about what the house would look like, she was unprepared for how terrible it was . . . much worse than she'd ever imagined. Its state of deterioration was unbelievable and looked like something out of a horror movie. Her eyes were immediately drawn to the considerable number of holes in the floor, making her question how safe it would be to step inside and walk around. She foolishly hadn't asked the attorney any questions about the house's age, its condition, or how long it had been since her mother lived there. In fact, she wasn't even sure her mother had actually ever lived in the house. The attorney hadn't been very helpful or forthcoming either . . . never offering any substantial information about the house. He had matter-of-factly stated, "Your momma left the Texas house to you alone . . . as is." Why hadn't she followed up and asked for details about what the "as is" meant? If she had then, maybe she'd be better prepared now. But again, like many other issues, it was too late.

As Kendra walked carefully through the house— searching for something . . . anything worthwhile—she stepped around holes, sinking floor boards, loose pieces of linoleum, and chunks of fallen ceiling material.

The nasty smell lingered throughout the house but more so in the kitchen area . . . most likely because of the numerous holes throughout the small space. Kendra was unable to keep from thinking about what might be dead or alive below the floor boards, but no way did she want to find out . . . the possibilities too revolting to contemplate.

Feeling she'd spent too much time on the empty rooms and knowing the sun would be setting soon, she needed to find the attic as soon as possible. Before leaving the kitchen, Kendra took one last look around—thinking thoughtfully—someone once lived there . . . maybe her mother or maybe not. Either way, the house was utterly disgusting. Even if fixed up, it was sad to think of anyone living such an isolated life out there . . . miles from nowhere.

When walking through the house, she'd already looked at each room's ceiling for some sort of attic access. While looking, she'd also thought about how she'd get through a ceiling opening without a ladder. With mixed emotions, she was somewhat relieved when no possible opening was discovered.

Since the attic was the main reason for visiting the house in the first place, she'd obviously missed something on the walk-through. Perhaps she'd been distracted while cautiously taking each and every step . . . mindful of falling and getting hurt.

Reconsidering, the only other possibility—not inspected earlier—was a narrow door across from a small room . . . presumed to be a bedroom. Since the door didn't have a lock on it, she'd dismissed it, guessing it was a storage closet. Not bothering to open the door; it couldn't be what she was looking for—a door needing a small key to open—and had quickly moved on.

Returning to the door, it opened easily and to her surprise, she faced stairs leading upward. Backing up, the thought of climbing them without any light would be scary . . . even impossible. Most likely, the steps were in the same disrepair as the rest of the house. Unnoticed before, good thing a light switch was beside the door. Quickly flipping the switch upward, there was no response. Darn it . . . another question not asked to her mother's attorney, "Would the utilities be on?" Naturally, he couldn't have answered her, because he didn't know when she'd be coming. After seeing the house for herself, the attorney most likely would have told her not to go to the house alone, not to be there close to dark, and given her other sensible suggestions. Today, she couldn't have argued with any of his remarks, because they would have been rational and totally correct . . . leading her to realize what a dummy she'd been while being spontaneous.

Tired and emotional about leaving without seeing what was in the attic—if anything or nothing—it dawned on her to use the light from the cell phone to guide her. Without checking out the attic, she knew this trip would be another utter failure. Disgusted, it would be one more failure to add to her list of many others. But, as her therapist often said, "Failure is never a good option." So, nothing ventured, nothing gained kept going through her mind.

Encouraged, Kendra pointed the phone toward the stairs. Full of anticipation, she still couldn't keep from worrying about making it safely to the top and hopefully the attic. As she climbed upward, Kendra held the phone in one hand and slid the other hand's fingers against the wall for balance. While touching the wall and hearing the boards squeak beneath each step, her body began to quiver. Aware of the hair standing up on both arms, she had a sudden eerie feeling of somehow being there before. How ridiculous was that . . . even impossible. With each upward step, she began talking to herself out loud, "You can do this. You need to get to the attic. It's going to be okay." Then repeating, "I can do this. I can do this. I can do this."

Kendra eventually found herself standing on a small platform at the top of the stairs—directly in front of a similar door to the one downstairs—only this one had a lock with a small keyhole. Knowing she'd be in complete darkness without the phone's light, she reminded herself of using precious phone battery and should get in and out as quickly as possible. While not knowing the exact time, she did know that the few rays of sunshine still above the horizon wouldn't last much longer.

Hesitating a moment before inserting the key and realizing she'd been holding her breath, Kendra let out a sigh and opened the door. Surprised, the room was small and completely closed in like a big walk-in closet. It was nothing like what she'd expected the attic to look like . . . not like the attics she'd seen in movies with open floor boards and the underside of the roof showing. The room was dimly lit with the only light coming in from a small window facing west. It had the same strong smell as the kitchen, but there were no visible holes in the floor. If she'd needed to describe the area to another person, she'd say it was smaller than a typical small room but larger than a big walk-in closet. Finding the repulsive odor difficult to inhale, Kendra worked her way toward the window . . . navigating around a few boxes, a child's highchair, and a metal trunk. When sliding the highchair off to the side, the strange sensation she'd encountered while climbing the stairs returned. Shaking her head, the creepy feeling made no sense.

Reaching the window—wanting . . . no needing to open it to allow fresh air to enter—Kendra was grateful for the faint light still entering the room. Regardless of how many times she tried to slide the lock out of the rusted slot, the window just wouldn't budge. Unable to release the lock, she placed both hands against the top of the window and tried to jerk it back and forth. As ripples of perspiration trickled down her face, she wiped her brow before noticing her hands were filthy . . . thinking, now her face was smeared with dirt. "Yuck!"

Frustrated, Kendra knew she'd run out of time. No way could she take care of the attic today. Disappointed, the thought of coming back sickened her. Turning to leave and thinking about the best way to proceed tomorrow, she stepped on something hard. Looking down and even in the fading light, a dead rat was sprawled out on the dusty floor. Well, now she knew where the disgusting odor was coming from. Quickly stepping away from the dead animal with its blank stare and open mouth, Kendra scanned the floor for other dead rats or possible live ones. She didn't see any but did notice holes near the box bottoms, leading her to first wonder and then assume there were rat nests inside.

While hurrying down the stairs—as carefully as possible—she eventually reached the bottom step. Realizing she'd forgotten to lock the attic door during her rushed exit, there was no way she was going back up there. Well, probably tomorrow but definitely not tonight. Exhausted, she began to cry. Not caring about her dirty fingers, Kendra did her best to wipe the tears away.

Standing on the porch and still using the cell phone for light, Kendra moved cautiously down the front steps. Thinking about what was next on her non-existent agenda, she needed to find the small town of Sabinal. Of course, that would require retracing the drive back to the road where she'd veered off to follow the attorney's directions.

It had been a difficult drive with sunlight; now it would be especially tricky. Oh well, if she could survive driving here, walking through the house, and finding the attic—with or without rats—then she could survive anything.

Starting the car, what if Sabinal didn't have a hotel? Hum, if the town had an attorney's office; surely it would have at least one hotel or motel.

Chapter 2

Taking a moment to realize where she was, Kendra woke disoriented and uncomfortable. Blinking a few times and wondering what time it was, she slowly reached for her phone. Opening her eyes wider and blinking again, it was hard to believe it was almost ten o'clock. Wow, she couldn't remember ever sleeping in that late, but after the stress of yesterday's terrible drive and shocking house . . . it made perfect sense.

When entering Sabinal last night, she'd picked this motel for three reasons. It was the first motel she saw, the vacancy sign was lit-up, and there was a diner next door. As she'd turned into the parking lot, it seemed like a good idea to check-in and then go to the diner to eat. However, by the time she'd gotten into the room, all she could think about was going to bed.

Barely unpacking—removing only the absolute necessities—Kendra had finally slipped under the covers. Almost asleep, she thought about how the phone's light had helped her reach the attic, and how she couldn't have managed without it. While appreciating the phone's help, it suddenly dawned on her . . . she'd forgotten to charge it. Reluctantly forcing herself to get back up, she dug through her purse until finding the charger. Constantly yawning while searching around the room for an outlet, she eventually found one directly below the small table next to the bed. That's convenient, she'd thought . . . wishing she'd started looking there first, so she could have returned to bed sooner.

Still not fully awake but realizing it was already late, Kendra knew that plans should be made right away about what needed to be accomplished today. Should she call the attorney now and set up a time to meet or shower and dress before making the call? Her old self would have already scheduled the entire day, but this trip was nothing like her normal routine—not even close—and duly noted from day one; or as her therapist called it . . . her adventurous journey.

Even though feeling both grimy from traveling and from being inside that filthy house; she was also extremely hungry, realizing she hadn't eaten since early yesterday. No way could she go next door for breakfast without first taking a shower. It seemed like an easy decision to quickly shower, dress, and then go to breakfast. She could contact the attorney from the diner. It was a minor plan—a spur-of-the-moment decision—so felt she was still being spontaneous.

Stepping into the shower, it hit her that her inner clock was still on California time, so actually she woke a little before eight o'clock. But what if her phone hadn't automatically adjusted to Texas time? It could be even worse . . . two hours ahead and almost noon.

Most likely, the front office clerk would think she was stupid, but she'd call anyway and ask for the correct time. Once she knew the exact time, she could decide on the best way to proceed. Remember, she told herself; you can do this and survive without second guessing every move you make . . . so here goes.

"Good morning," was answered pleasantly; followed quickly by, "How can I help you?"

"Well, this might sound silly but can you tell me what time it is?"

"Of course ma'am . . . it's 10:25 and today is Friday. You should have a clock radio in your room, and it should be set to Texas time."

Feeling somewhat foolish, Kendra paused to look around for a clock but didn't see one.

"Can I help you with anything else?" the clerk asked.

"No, that's all I needed to know. Thank you."

"You're welcome, and y'all have a blessed day."

Kendra placed the phone down but couldn't rid herself of that familiar sensation of negativity. And even though the clerk was pleasant, Kendra was certain the lady considered her not very bright. Why else would she tell her the day of the week in addition to the time, and why mention a clock in the room? She should have told her there was no clock radio available. What if she left and they thought she's taken it. Once dressed, she reminded herself not to return to her old ways of thinking the worst of every situation and over-reacting. Maybe the clerk told her the day because people flying in from other countries can lose or gain hours . . . even days. She remembered adjusting to a lost day when traveling to Europe a few years back. As her therapist often said, "Don't sweat the small stuff and don't make something out of nothing." Smiling, she'd thought a lot about her therapist's advice while on this trip. Smiling again, "Nothing ventured . . . nothing gained" came to mind—remembered from a recent session. However, the verdict was still out on any gain coming from this traveling venture.

Feeling much better and just before leaving for the diner, she walked past the television set. Oddly enough, she hadn't turned it on . . . a definite first. Usually, when entering a hotel room for the first time, it was a priority to make sure the television and remote functioned properly. But then, this was her first time to stay in a motel instead of a hotel. Another first, and even in her exhausted state the previous night, she was proud of herself for getting the large and heavy suitcase out of the trunk of the car and into the room without help.

As she paused to think about last night and the television, it seemed like a better idea to retrieve the attorney's telephone number from her wallet while in the room—where it was quiet—than at the diner, where she might need to wait for a table.

Locating the attorney's business card, Kendra changed her mind again, deciding to call him from the room. Whether for better or worse, changing her mind was becoming a familiar choice for her new way of life. So, before calling, she told herself . . . even though I can do change, I want to learn how to be good at it. All of my life, I've done exactly what Mother said I should do . . . never close to what I wanted to do. Now, the reality has become both scary and freeing.

After three rings, she listened to the following message: "You have reached the law office of John T. Blevins. The office is currently closed. Normal business hours are Monday through Thursday, ten a.m. until five p.m. unless out attending court. After the beep, please leave a brief message and your telephone number. Your call will be returned as soon as possible."

Not sure how to respond, Kendra momentarily froze when hearing the beep and disconnected the call. What to do now? She felt like screaming. Afraid of having a panic attack, she began going through her breathing exercises . . . feeling her heart pounding with each deep breath. In order to keep the attack from becoming debilitating, she was supposed to focus on something pleasant. However, visions of the countless holes in the floors of that dreadful house kept overwhelming her thoughts.

From past experiences and familiar with the panic attack process, Kendra knew she should take an anxiety pill, lie down, and continue to take slow deep breaths. Noticing the prescription bottle among the items removed from her purse earlier, she got a glass of water and quickly downed a pill. Although months had passed since needing to take any medication—not even aspirin—she still felt more secure knowing she had the medicine with her in case of a problem occurring . . . like now.

Soon after placing her head on the pillow, the heart racing began to ease . . . or was it her imagination? Obviously, the pill did not have time to work. But then, her stomach was empty. From past experiences, she'd learned that part of confronting a panic attack was also to concentrate on a different situation—like a new project— especially if unable to go to a happy place. How strange, not even walking through that dilapidated house had affected her this way. Perhaps, concentrating on finding the attic had given her purpose and garnered her complete attention. Beginning to feel a bit calmer, what present project could she do?

A no-brainer, she needed to put on her big girl pants, call the attorney's office and—this time for sure—leave a message. Okay, she could do this. She'd tackled a lot of new experiences during the last few days and shouldn't surrender to her insecurities now. Making room on the small table, her immediate project was to write down exactly what she wanted to say—word for word—when calling his office again.

When hearing the beep, she began, "My name is Kendra Smith. My mother, Christine Smith, left me a house in Sabinal. I am in Sabinal today . . . ah, Friday. I've traveled all the way from California to meet with Mr. Blevins and didn't know the office would be closed today. I'm hoping there is some way I can meet with Mr. Blevins or at least speak with him today? Please call me back as soon as possible." After giving her phone number, Kendra nervously whispered, "Thank you."

After leaving the "not brief" message, Kendra felt surprisingly better but again returned to thinking about what she should have done or not have done before driving to Texas. Regardless of it being her own fault for placing herself in this situation and not using better judgment, this panic attack was strangely milder than others she'd experienced in the past. Perhaps there was hope for her after all. Either way, it is what it is, and she'd go eat instead of continuing to dwell on something impossible to change.

Worst case scenario, there would be no return call until the office opened on Monday. And even though her feelings had gone from anger, to panic, to finally resolve, she was still hungry. Observing her present emotions as progress, she picked up her purse, grabbed the room key, and set off for the diner.

Fearing she wouldn't be back before check-out time, Kendra stopped at the motel office to register for another day and mentioning the possibility of needing to stay additional days. Before exiting the office, she firmly said, "By the way, I do not have a clock in my room."

Finishing a plate of pancakes, bacon, and hash browns—fattening food items never allowed while growing up and then avoided as an adult—Kendra motioned for the check. While thanking the waitress and giving her a nice tip, the phone rang. Not sure of the number but aware it had a Texas prefix, she hesitantly answered, "Hello."

"Is this Kendra Smith?" the caller inquired.

Worried about it being a scam call and without answering "Yes" or "No," Kendra asked, "Who's calling?"

"My name is Timothy Blevins. I'm returning a message for my daddy at our law office. Am I speaking with Kendra Smith?"

"Yes, I am Kendra Smith, and I left the message," she answered in a direct manner.

"So . . . if I understand your message, you are presently in Sabinal to discuss the property left to you by your mother? Am I correct?"

"Yes, I talked to Mr. Blevins . . . ah, your father, some time ago but didn't say when I'd be coming to Sabinal."

"Unfortunately, my daddy is on vacation. You could say I'm filling in for him if an unforeseen problem arises. Our office is actually located in Uvalde, but we still service folks in Sabinal when needed."

"So if I understand you correctly; I won't be able to meet with your father until he returns from vacation?"

Before he could reply, Kendra asked, "When will he be back?"

"He'll be gone for at least another week . . . maybe longer."

Feeling the hairs standing up on her arms, Kendra told herself to be in control and took a couple of deep breaths. "So, do you have a suggestion for me? I've already been to the house. It's in dreadful condition. I tried to check out the contents in the attic, but it got late and almost dark outside. I had no choice but to leave."

"Knowing you've traveled a long distance, I understand your dilemma. On a good note, I just had a long conversation with my daddy, John Blevins. If you're willing, I would be happy to meet with you."

Hesitating before replying, Kendra asked, "Are you saying you'd meet me at the house or just meet me somewhere to talk?"

"Well, I'm thinking . . . since you've come so far, and my daddy told me your mother was adamant for you to see the contents of the attic, I could accompany to back to the house. Before you answer, I couldn't do it today. If I can be so bold, I have the weekend free and could meet with you tomorrow. Oh, and before I forget, my daddy has a letter addressed to you from your mother. It's in our company safe. When he received the letter, the instructions were very clear. It was to be given to you—and only to you—unopened until after her passing."

Trying to take it all in, Kendra didn't immediately reply.

When there was no response, Timothy paused before uttering, "Forgive me for not saying how sorry I am for your loss. With your permission, I can give the letter to you, go over the disposition of the house, and help you navigate through the legal process."

Kendra answered quickly, "Yes . . . that would really be appreciated, but where would we do this? Trust me . . . there's no place at the house to do any of that."

After oddly chuckling, he answered, "By the way, my daddy emphatically told me not to let you go to the house unaccompanied. Now that I know you've already been there; it seems a tad late to bring that up. So, what are your wishes . . . ah, is it Miss Smith or Mrs. Smith?"

"It's Miss Smith," Kendra answered, wondering why he asked and why he cared.

"Well, Miss Smith, let's talk about a good place to meet and talk."

After discussing several places to talk—all unknown to Kendra—Timothy Blevins offered, "How about we have breakfast tomorrow at the diner where you are now . . . my treat, and I'll bring your mother's letter. You choose the best time for you."

"Well, I've noticed the diner slows down here about ten, but it will be Saturday."

"Sounds good! Ten o'clock tomorrow morning . . . it is. That will give me plenty of time to go by the office, pick up the letter, and drive to Sabinal."

"But you'll still go with me to the house . . . won't you?" Kendra questioned in an almost pleading manner.

"Of course," he answered before adding, "See you tomorrow. I'm looking forward to meeting you, Miss Smith."

Heading back to the motel, Kendra felt surprisingly up-lifted. If everything fell into place, she could be on her way back to California tomorrow.

Chapter 3

Before leaving to meet Timothy Blevins, Kendra packed her suitcase and stopped at the office to settle the bill. That way, she'd be able to leave from her mother's house and be a few miles closer to home. In spite of the many reasons for not wanting to return to that awful place, scrutinizing the items in the attic would be the last time to confront the house's existence and bring closure to her mother's wishes. Gratefully, it would be easier this time; she wouldn't be alone.

Parking the car in front of the diner, Kendra ignored her desire to become good at change, so returned to her old ways of being early for an appointment. Looking down at her watch, she was right on time . . . exactly ten minutes early. Regardless of what she kept telling herself to do or be, in reality she hadn't quite conquered the numerous areas that needed improvement. I'm getting closer but not quite where I hoped to be, she pensively thought.

Her last thoughts before entering the diner . . . I am in control, and I can do this. Having no clue about the person she'd be meeting—his age or appearance—and before telling the hostess she would be waiting for someone; a nicely dressed gentleman stood up behind a nearby table—seemingly smiling directly at her. If the person she was meeting was indeed the man looking at her, he too was early for their appointment. Not only did she find that interesting, but he also gave the impression that he recognized her . . . as the person he was waiting to meet. Without smiling back and after taking a deep breath, she thought . . . I am in control. I can do this . . . here goes.

In spite of her emotional and significant physical make-over during the past months, Kendra still worried about how her clothes looked, if she'd applied the correct make-up, and if her shoes were appropriate for the occasion. Just because she'd lately been told how great she looked and had received constant compliments, she still felt unattractive . . . especially when meeting someone new. As Kendra walked in his direction, she felt embarrassed and that old feeling of being judged returned. She knew he was following her movements so tried not to look directly at him. Better to concentrate on each step forward and focus on not tripping.

With her hand extended, Kendra inquired in a forthright manner, "Are you Timothy Blevins?"

"Yes ma'am, but you can call me Tim or Timothy. I'm assuming you are Miss Smith."

Nodding in the affirmative, she offered a short, "Yes."

Getting the awkward introductions out of the way, Kendra appreciated his nice manners as he held the chair out for her. Their conversation was guarded at first until Timothy began to chat about joining his daddy's law practice and how his daddy kept talking about retirement.

"If the truth be known, I don't think my daddy really wants to give it up. I think he's pretty well decided to work off and on, taking vacations often and whenever it pleases him. Hence, his present fishing trip to the Gulf of Mexico."

To her surprise, Kendra learned that John Blevins had been her mother's attorney for a long time . . . many years even. She thought about asking how many years but decided not to. However, during this initial conversation, Kendra offered, "I didn't know the house even existed until your father contacted me. My mother never volunteered anything about her past. In fact, she outright refused to discuss it." Inwardly chastising herself, she shouldn't have said anything and clearly shouldn't have any follow up to her remark. She obviously didn't want to open herself up to discussing or answering any uncomfortable questions. No one— except for her therapist—knew what she'd gone through, and she wanted it to stay that way.

Neither of them volunteered anything additional about their personal lives. However, Kendra's comment about her mother's outright refusal to discuss her past did not pass by unnoticed. Even though curious, Tim didn't feel comfortable about pursuing her remark . . . telling himself, this is our first meeting and in reality, it's none of my business now or later.

Finishing a nice breakfast of a vegetable omelet and toast . . . no pancakes this time, Kendra watched Timothy finish a huge plate of grits, eggs rancheros, and sausage. Both had orange juice and coffee. When she commented on how hungry he must have been, he answered with a grin, "No, this is just a normal meal for me." His remark caused her to wonder how he could appear so fit, yet normally eat so much food.

As the waitress cleared the table, Kendra asked where the girl's bathroom was located and excused herself . . . purposely leaving before Timothy could help her out of the chair.

When Timothy saw Kendra returning, he moved his briefcase aside, stood, and helped her with the chair again. After she was settled, he asked, "Do you want to open the letter now or would you prefer to read it later in the privacy of your room?"

Momentarily taken aback, she'd forgotten all about the letter. Perhaps she'd been fixated on returning to the house again, seeing the contents of the attic, and driving back to California.

"I guess I should read it now before we leave." After saying that, she thought . . . how bad could it be?

Receiving the envelope—obviously placed on the table while she'd been away—Kendra was surprised by its large size . . . noticing the manila envelope was taped shut and hand addressed by her mother. Embarrassed by her trembling fingers as she tried to open it, she paused briefly.

Feeling like he was intruding into a private moment, Timothy offered, "I'll be right back."

Kendra watched him walk in the direction of the bathrooms, thinking how comfortable she was beginning to feel with him . . . a perfect stranger. Baby steps, she thought. After all, he was the first man she'd been alone with—one-on-one—since the incident happened. She momentarily visited that dark place before being distracted by a little girl's giggling at a nearby table. Eventually tearing open the envelope, she was confused by the contents. There were three standard size business letters inside. Each one had her name written on it, along with the numbers: #1, #2, and #3.

While cautiously opening the first letter (#1), she glanced up to see Timothy paying for their breakfast. To her surprise, the letter was fairly short . . . constantly begging for her forgiveness. It rambled on and on about how it had been her fault for the dreadful life she'd caused her only daughter to endure. Kendra reread the brief letter several times, trying her best to understand exactly what her mother was talking about. Bottom line, the letter didn't make a whole lot of sense. Perhaps the therapist could help interpret it for her when she returned to California.

Letter (#2's) first sentence read as follows: Please do not read more of this letter until after seeing the contents of the trunk in the attic at the Sabinal house. Perhaps and hopefully, my life and your life will make more sense after that. Again, I beg for your forgiveness.

Kendra meticulously returned the first and second letters to their corresponding envelopes. Gathering the three letters together, she placed all of them back into the manila envelope. After safely storing everything into her purse, Kendra waved for Timothy to join her. She knew he'd been meandering near the cashier's station in order to give her more time and space to read her mother's letter. Even though he didn't know there were three instead of one, his actions of not rushing her seemed considerate . . . even sensitive. Unbelievably nice, she thought . . . but why?

"Are you okay?" he questioned on his return.

"Yes, thank you," she answered quickly, trying to convey being in control.

While still standing, Timothy asked, "So . . . are we off?"

"Yes, I'm ready, Kendra replied with a sincere smile."

Walking through the exit door, Kendra turned in the direction of her parked car. As she did, she realized she'd parked where Timothy had a clear view from the diner of her and the car's California license plate. Now understanding his immediate attention to her earlier when entering the restaurant, she heard Tim's voice say, "Hey . . . wait up! Aren't we going together?"

Knowing she was frowning, Kendra turned and said, "That's not possible. I plan to return to California after leaving the house . . . hopefully for the last time."

"Well, let's talk about this a moment. When I talked to my daddy, he said I should stop by his house and drive his pickup out to the house. He said getting to the house would be difficult at best, because it would be slow going on bad roads. I just assumed we'd be going together. Isn't that what you meant when you asked if I'd go with you?"

"Well yes, but I was thinking we'd go in separate cars. When we finished, you could then go back to Uvalde, and I could leave for California. I've already checked out of the motel."

"That's fine, but do you know how to get there from here, because I don't."

"Well, I still have the directions on the way to the house, but I followed the signs leading to Sabinal after leaving the house."

"So here's the deal. I jotted down the directions my daddy gave me . . . from here to there. Honestly, my daddy wasn't exactly sure and guessed sometimes on the turns. If I understand you correctly, your plan is to leave the house and go back the same way you came? Were the roads okay on your way to the house?"

"No . . . not really. In fact, they were awful. I really don't want to go back the same way but thought it would be faster since I'd be closer."

"Maybe we should go back inside and discuss this further. I was thinking between the two of us and my dad's directions, we could find the house together. In my opinion it seems better for you to leave your car here, go with me to the house, come back here to pick up your car, and then leave for California. It might be a few miles longer, but you can take Highway 90 straight out of Sabinal towards

California. In the long run, it will save you time and would definitely be much safer."

Realizing he was making good sense, Kendra could feel both hands beginning to quiver.

Noticing her hands were shaking, Timothy asked, "Are you okay?"

"Sorta," she answered before hesitantly adding, "No, not really."

"I'm sorry if I've upset you. I'm just here to help facilitate your mother's affairs—ah . . . now yours. I'll do whatever you wish. I'm sorry if I've overstepped and put you in an uncomfortable position."

"No, it's not that. Everything is changing for me and . . . ."

Timothy answered, "Understood," but really didn't. "Speaking along those lines, there are also papers that will need to be signed before a notary. I guess we can talk about that after we visit the house. If you'd rather not, then I guess it can be discussed over the phone later. I can even send the paperwork to you. Once returned, it wouldn't be a problem for my daddy or myself to file them at the recorder's office."

Receiving no response, Timothy continued, "Sorry . . . more changes. Please don't stress, we'll get this done. There are lots of options to consider."

When he looked directly into her face, subtle tears glistened in the sunlight. "You're not okay. Please tell me what I can do to help?"

"I'm the one who's sorry. Guess I'm kinda a mess. This is all so new to me."

"Well, according to my original plan, I'd talk about the house after you had a better idea of your options and then proceed accordingly. Is there a big rush for you to return to California?"

"No . . . not really, other than I feel more comfortable at home. Like I said before; this house situation is all new to me." What she wanted to say was that returning to her apartment was a form of hiding away with very few decisions to make. "This is taking a lot longer than I previously considered. Please don't misunderstand . . . it's my fault for thinking I'd get here Thursday, take care of business Thursday or Friday at the latest, and already be back on my way home."

"May I make a suggestion?"

"Of course, you can."

"Okay! I'm thinking that you want to get as much settled as possible while you're here, so you won't need to return. Am I right?"

With a nod from Kendra, he continued, "Please stop me if you disagree while I'm throwing out possibilities. Let's go together to the house in my daddy's pickup. Then, we'll come back here and get your car. You can follow me to Uvalde to the office where we can finalize the paperwork. I'll see if I can find a notary. Since today is Saturday, that may or may not be possible. Worst case scenario, you'll spend the night in Uvalde and leave refreshed tomorrow."

Kendra tried to listen to what he was saying but was fixated on changing her plans to leave today. Everything was so messed up.

"What if I can't find a place to stay in Uvalde?" she asked.

"Trust me . . . that won't be a problem."

"What about my car? Will it be safe here in the parking lot?"

"Sure . . . no problem."

"Your suggestions do seem feasible . . . maybe even better. But what if a notary can't be found on Saturday or Sunday? Then . . . what?"

"That's possible but if not in a rush to get home, you'll be able to relax and enjoy a bit more of our Texas hospitality."

"Just a moment, I need to get something out of my car."

Confused, Timothy asked, "Do you need some help?"

"No, I'll be right back."

As he watched her remove a paper sack from the car's back seat, he wasn't exactly sure what to think of her. She seemed like a cowed puppy dog—timid and vulnerable— yet extremely bright and thoughtful. Oh well, maybe he'd have time to have a more personal discussion with her during the drive, but only if she volunteered for the conversation to go in that direction.

When Kendra returned—carrying the sack with handles—he smiled before asking, "Is that lunch?"

Wanting to quip . . . surely you're not hungry after pigging out, but instead answered, "No, they're items I should have taken to the house last time . . . bottles of water, wash clothes, and a couple of flashlights. Oh, and I brought a first aid kit too."

"Good for you," answered quickly before continuing along that same line. "My daddy told me to be sure and take a shovel and branch cutters . . . reminding me to take care of "his baby." That's his pet name for the pickup." Pointing in the opposite direction, "It's the red job over yonder. Follow me."

As Timothy opened the truck's door and Kendra faced a big step upward, she was glad she'd worn tennis shoes and loose workout pants. When dressing this morning and even though purposely color-coordinating her outfit, she had concentrated on addressing the run-down house and stairs. It had been a good decision—easy and practical—not to wear tight designer pants and open toed shoes this time to the house. Although changing her apparel to confront the house again, she was now happy for a second reason . . . the daunting big step up into the pickup's front seat. Concentrating on stepping up without falling backwards, she was appreciative of Tim's help . . . balancing her arm below the elbow and bracing his other hand against her lower back. Oh my God, she had that same tingly feeling she'd had when Albert first touched her. Swallowing, she told herself not to go there, to concentrate on the red dashboard and the long matching red seat, and for God's sake . . . do not to have a panic attack.

Settling down on the hard seat and taking back the paper sack, she quietly mumbled, "Thank you," but wasn't sure if Timothy heard her. When she looked back in his direction, he'd already closed the door and was quickly walking around to the driver's side.

Not used to driving without conversing, Timothy began to describe the old town and point out places of interest . . . which he admitted . . . were few and far between.

Unable to think of a good response or any response, Kendra reminded herself of the therapist telling her to look at the trip as a new adventure.

When leaving the city limits, Kendra offered, "This is the first time I've ridden in a pickup."

"The first time in a pickup or the first time in an old pickup like this one?" he questioned with a wide smile.

"First time for both," she replied quickly. "It's amazing and nothing like the front seat of a car."

"That's for sure. Newer pickups have bucket seats like cars. I think this front seat is called a bench seat. I'm not even sure what all of the knobs on the dashboard mean. Per Daddy, it's been restored to its original sixty's grandeur. Naturally, this is his pride-and-joy. I think he's more proud of this old truck than anything else. Don't get me wrong; I'm not against old things but prefer being comfortable first. Sorry for the hard seat."

Not commenting on the seat—which indeed felt like sitting on a thick board—she had already thought about how it would feel when the road became bumpy and rough. Wanting to say something nice about the truck, she offered, "Your father's truck has the biggest steering wheel I've ever seen. I don't think I could see over it to drive or even reach the pedals." Looking downward, Kendra shook her head before adding, "My feet don't even touch the floor on the passenger side."

The good news of talking about the pickup, she'd been able to move her attention away from Albert and that negative memory. Grateful not to be behind the wheel or driving this time to the house, Kendra began to somewhat relax and concentrated on the passing scenery.

Chapter 4

After several wrong turns, they arrived at the spot where Kendra had previously scratched her car.

"I see now what you were talking about," Timothy stated matter-of-factly. "I better get out and do some clean-up before we continue."

Watching Timothy go to the backend of the pickup, drop something down that made a loud thud, and then remove several tools; she marveled at his willingness to help her. His demeanor continued to amaze her . . . finding it easy to enjoy his company. If she followed her mother's sentiments, men were only after one thing and could never, ever be trusted. Well, she'd veered away from that sinister perspective when meeting Albert and look how that turned out.

As she watched Timothy clip away at the dried bushes, she tried to understand why he was being so nice, wondering if he, his father, or both were gaining financially for his helpfulness. As he moved to the other side of the opening and began clipping again—closer to her side—she had a better view of him. While his attention was directed at the dry brush—she could easily stare at him without either of them feeling uncomfortable.

Kendra began to speculate about his background, his age, and if he had family . . . other than a father. Although curious, how could she ask questions without answering similar questions he might ask in return? Her thoughts were interrupted when Timothy turned and walked over to the pickup's window, asking, "How about some of that water you brought?"

As he watched Kendra dig into the sack on the floorboard, he added, "Gosh, I can't believe how out of shape I've become. Growing up, my summer jobs were full of mowing yards, clipping hedges, and even digging ditches. I hope my daddy will be pleased that I've kept his baby out of harm's way."

"Well, I'm impressed with your hard work, and I'm sure your father will also be appreciative. I'll be your witness at court if you need one," Kendra replied with a big smile.

After finishing the water and handing the empty bottle back, he offered, "I'll put the tools back, and then we can continue on our merry way."

Pushing the tailgate back into place, Timothy momentarily fixated on Kendra's smile. He was finding her more curious than ever, wishing he'd gotten more information about her from his daddy. He found it extremely odd that she hadn't volunteered anything— absolutely nothing—about herself along the way.

When the pickup started, Kendra suddenly remembered worrying about her car starting; realizing she hadn't considered what would happen if the pickup didn't start. Hating the thought of returning to that awful place, she sighed before saying, "It's not far from here."

As they stopped in front of the house, Timothy remarked quietly, "Oh . . . my."

"Wait 'til you see the inside. It's incredibly awful. Remember . . . be very careful where you step."

"Hang on and I'll help you out of the truck and carry the sack too," he offered.

"Okay, but I think I can make it." However, as she glanced out the window and down at the ground, she changed her mind before saying, "On second thought, I should wait for you."

By the time Timothy arrived at her side and opened the door, Kendra had already picked up the sack, noticing the flashlights were still near the top for easy access. Maneuvering up the porch steps and entering again through the front door, Kendra asked, "So, what do you think?"

"Your description was right on, and the smell is beyond sickening . . . if that's possible."

"Well, get ready because it gets worse in the attic. I saw at least one dead rat up there. In fact, I even stepped on it. It was so gross."

Scrunching his nose in disgust, Timothy asked, "Which way to the attic? Lay on, Macduff."

"I see you're a student of Shakespeare," Kendra quipped. "Most would say, 'Lead on, Macduff.'"

"I'm thinking most wouldn't have a clue about Macbeth or Shakespeare anymore. You, however, impressed me with your statistical knowledge during our drive."

"Flattery won't get you out of here any quicker," she replied and grinned. "Do you want to look around the house first?"

"No, but thank you for asking. I've seen enough already."

"Okay, but part of the ambiance is seeing the multitude of holes in the floor and the collapsing ceilings—not to mention the smell is stronger in some of the other rooms, especially in the kitchen area . . . more holes there."

"I'll take your word for it, and again I'll pass."

Kendra was surprised . . . even shocked that she was actually having fun kibitzing with him. How could this be happening in such an awful place? Better yet . . . how could this be happening at all? Before opening the door leading to the stairs, she handed Timothy a flashlight.

As they climbed the stairs, she waited for that strange feeling from before to reappear—but it didn't. It must have been her imagination; or perhaps she felt safer now with Timothy close by. She watched as he opened the attic door and carefully pushed it inward. His spontaneous reaction was expected, but his words were unexpected. "Oh my God . . . this is what was so important for you to come all this way to see?"

"I guess," answered hesitantly. "Perhaps not important looking to us but must have been important to Mother. I'm thinking that what's inside the metal trunk is what she really wanted me to see. Now you can understand why I couldn't stay here when it was almost dark."

"Well, the stench alone is enough to make a person want to hightail it out of here. Hang on a minute while I open the window."

"Good luck with that. I couldn't."

Kendra watched as he tried several times to loosen it. She wished she'd brought something to help free it—or at the very least—explained the probability of needing something to open the window before leaving. The old Kendra would have gone over and over every possible scenario and been more prepared but again . . . too late.

"Okay, I'll be right back," Timothy offered in a frustrated manner. Since noticing her hands shaking since entering the attic, he asked, "Will you be alright while I go down to the truck?"

"Yes, but be careful." Having said that, she was not only worried about him having a problem but also selfishly thinking about herself if something happened to him.

When he returned, he was carrying a metal toolbox. After some pounding with a hammer and screwdriver—which she actually recognized—the window was up and fresh air rushed in.

Seemingly relieved and not bothered by his dirty hands, Timothy asked, "What would you like to tackle first?" Without an immediate answer, he followed with, "I'm sure you've given it a lot of thought."

"Yes, I actually have. Could we open the boxes first and get them out of the way? There aren't very many and fairly small. I'd like to open the metal trunk last. Is that okay with you?"

"Of course it is," was answered with a tilted head and confused look.

The first box was stuffed to the top with chewed-up baby clothes and baby blankets . . . disgustingly full of rat droppings.

Baffled by the contents, Kendra wondered why her mother would have and then keep baby items. Possibilities flooded through her mind in an instant. Did her mother have another child? Could it have been given up for adoption? Did it possibly die, and that's why Mother never wanted to talk about her past? If any of these possibilities were true, why not just discuss the circumstances with her . . . especially as she became an adult. Looking at Timothy, all she could do was shake her head and raise her hands in bafflement.

The next box was half-full and contained household items: cheap silverware, unmatched dishes—many with chips or cracks—one pot, and one rusty skillet. Nothing matched, leading Kendra to question why anyone . . . especially her mother, would want to keep any of it.

The third box contained a tattered blanket and miscellaneous linen items. They had also been chewed on by rats . . . similar to the first box of baby clothes. Thoughts of why bother to keep any of these objects continued to race through her mind. They obviously weren't considered important enough to take with her, so why pack and then keep them at the house. Maybe all of this had nothing to do with her mother. Perhaps her mother never lived in this house . . . bringing up additional questions. Why in the world did she even own this house or bother to keep it through the years?

The last box—the one with a chewed hole at the bottom—proved more difficult to open than the others. It had been oddly taped closed with layers and layers of different types of tape. When finally opened, Kendra gingerly leaned backward and frowned. It appeared to have something big and furry inside.

"What the heck is that?" she asked.

Reaching for a long handled screwdriver, Timothy lifted a section up. Unable to determine what it was, he lifted it higher before the piece slipped away. Each time he lifted a section, it immediately split into several pieces. Unable to get enough out to determine what it was, Timothy finally answered, "I'm not sure what it is."

"It looks like some sort of fur to me," Kendra said before asking, "Do you know anything about animal fur?"

"Well, it kinda looks like a rabbit pelt to me. The fur is gray and black with streaks of white. It's similar to the rabbits we guys used to shoot on hunting trips."

"You killed a rabbit," she asked.

"Sure, we all did. It was something everyone did. It was no big deal back then."

"That's awful. How could you hurt a little helpless animal?"

Ignoring her question, he wondered why anyone would want to keep a rabbit pelt. It didn't make sense. But then . . . nothing about this place did. Taking a pair of pliers, he lifted a big section upward . . . trying to see how many pelts were in the box. When it was about half-way out, the top part separated and fell—fur side down—onto the floor.

Timothy stared at the piece of fur—still inside the pliers—noticing the back of the fur was not cured and tanned like a pelt would be. Instead, it was attached in a few places to a deteriorating fabric. At the same time, Kendra said, "I think it could be a jacket or coat." Looking closer at the piece on the floor, she added, "I think this is a collar." Bending over for a closer look, she continued, "There's a label with a picture of a rabbit, and it says Genuine Rabbit Fur."

"Would you like me to keep trying to get it all the way out?" Timothy inquired.

"No, I think we've seen enough."

"I agree. Also, if you're not fully convinced to stop, I'm pretty sure there's a couple of dead rats and a lot of poop just below the part I removed."

Not wanting to look inside the box again, Kendra said, "Let's move on to the metal trunk. I'm hoping that whatever's in it will be in better shape."

"I certainly hope so," was his quick response.

"Per mother's wishes, I'm not to finish her second letter until after seeing the contents of the trunk. I don't understand any of this."

"I'd like to help more, but I'm in the dark as much as you are," Timothy answered.

"I sure wish I knew what all of this means . . . the baby clothes, the highchair, and the rest of it. Do you think your father could enlighten us? Could you call and ask him?"

"Not from here. There's no phone service, cuz I've already checked."

"Oh, that's right. Well, maybe when we get back to town. I guess I better quit stalling and look into the trunk. Lord knows, I never want to come back here again . . . ever."

Timothy took Kendra's arm, helping her step over the fur pieces on the floor between them. Appreciative of the gesture and while thinking . . . perhaps chivalry is not dead, she said, "Thank you Sir Galahad."

When they stopped in front of the trunk, Timothy asked, "Do you have the key?"

Beginning to shake and feeling slightly nauseated, Kendra moved her head in a negative response.

"No problem . . . it's a small lock. I might have a bolt cutter in the toolbox."

As Timothy cut the lock and moved the latch to the side, Kendra felt herself holding her breath—which she'd been doing off and on since arriving—and waited for him to lift the top.

Tentative—yet curious—Kendra cautiously looked inside . . . instantly and thoroughly confused by what she saw. Because of her mother's refusal to discuss the past, it had shamefully crossed her mind that a dead baby might be found inside. With an abundance of relief and surprise, the trunk was almost empty, containing an assortment of different types and sizes of papers . . . maybe covering the bottom a few inches or so. From what little she could see, the papers were definitely hand-written by her mother and appeared to be randomly thrown inside.

Located on the top of the papers—approximately in the middle—was a single dead rose. Kendra reached in to move the dry rose aside for a better look below but changed her mind, deciding to pick it up. The rose immediately broke apart, the petals crumbling downward into what seemed like a hundred pieces. Feeling the rose had been left for her; she had destroyed it and began to sob.

Gaining some control and relieved that something awful wasn't found inside, it was still difficult to control the tears, or look at Timothy, or say anything. No way would he be able to understand what the rose meant to her.

Staring sadly at the scattered rose pieces, she could see partial bold letters directly beneath them. Ignoring the lettering and deciding to be sensible, her mother's second letter said not to continue until seeing the contents of the trunk . . . and she'd now done exactly that. At this point, all she wanted to do was close the trunk's lid and get away from the house.

Timothy's question, "Are you going to be okay?" brought her back to reality.

"I think so, but I'm not sure. Now that I've seen the contents of the trunk, I feel bad to just leave it here. It would take a long time to read what's in there, but I really want to leave."

"Would you mind if I make a suggestion?"

"Yes . . . ."

"Yes, you mind or . . . yes, it would be okay."

"Yes, any suggestion would be appreciated."

"I'm thinking the trunk doesn't seem heavy. I can put it in the truck, and you can read the contents when you decide to. Does that make sense?"

"It does. I'll help you pick up your stuff. I don't think either of us will ever want to come back to this awful place again. I'm pretty good at organizing. That's the least I can do."

"First, is there anything here—besides the trunk—that you want?"

"Heavens no!"

When Timothy leaned over to close the lid, he bumped into the trunk. As the rose pieces fell away and a good number moved off the page, bold letters appeared: **PLEASE READ IF YOU'VE FOUND THE ROSE.**

After reading the sentence, Timothy looked calmly at Kendra before saying, "You should read this before we go."

Answering, "What . . . I'm confused." Kendra leaned over and concentrated on the short sentence, reading it slowly and carefully . . . twice. Then read the following paragraph.

"Before I left, I buried something in front of the Cyprus tree—exactly ten feet from the porch corner post—in front of the house on the left side. I was angry when I did it, but you should dig it up the tin can before you leave. I'm sorry for not telling you in the second letter to bring a shovel."

Looking at Timothy, she asked, "Would you please read what she wrote?"

When finished, he offered, "That's no problem. Remember, I've dug ditches before, and I brought a shovel."

"Are you sure?" she questioned. "We can just leave."

"I think you'd always wonder. Let's clean-up here and put stuff away into the truck . . . not clean-up but you know what I mean."

"How can I ever thank you for all of your help and advice?"

Smiling, he answered, "I'll think of something."

Chapter 5

Kendra sat in the pickup more perplexed than ever. She kept looking at the diamond ring removed earlier from the tin can. The setting—a huge diamond in the center with slightly smaller diamonds on each side—looked like an expensive engagement ring . . . maybe an engagement ring or maybe not. Maybe it was real, or maybe it wasn't. Either way, it was gorgeous. In between touching and staring at the ring, she fixated on her mother's words about burying something before leaving. If thinking correctly, Mother's remark removed the possibility of whether or not her mother actually lived in the house. Well, not entirely. At the very least, she had been physically there but for how long. However, other unknowns still remained . . . like: why the baby stuff, why was the house still in her mother's name when she passed, and why did she keep the house through the years?

While Timothy was securing the metal trunk into the pickup's bed—learning that's what the back section is called—Kendra reached into her purse. Finding the #2 letter, she debated on whether to finish it now or wait until Timothy got back inside. While knowing him for only a short time, how odd to feel safe with him and value his opinions.

Unable to squelch her curiosity any longer, Kendra began to read the letter again until coming to the part where she'd stopped before at the restaurant. Sighing, she told herself . . . okay—per Mother's wishes—I've seen the contents of the trunk . . . so, here goes.

Hopefully, my dear, by now you've discovered the contents in the attic. I know you must have lots of questions. I also hope that you found the ring. It may seem unfair that I don't immediately reveal the mystery of what you've found there, but it is and always has been very complicated. I want you to realize that it will be much easier and clearer for you to understand once you read the papers found in the trunk. If I remember correctly, the papers were all dated, so putting them in order should help you figure out my past and some of yours. Regardless of what you decide to do, please know that I will love you always and forever. Again, I ask for your forgiveness.

After reading the entire letter again, Kendra heard Timothy opening the door. As he stepped into the truck and before asking if she was ready to go, the expression on her face—perplexed and strange—caught him off guard. "Uh-oh, please don't tell me we need to go back inside again," Timothy said before dropping his head. This time . . . it was his turn to sigh.

Although wanting to say more, Kendra gave him a short, "No" for an answer.

"Well, that's good, cuz I'm really getting hungry."

"Did it go okay with washing up?" Kendra asked.

"Yes, thanks . . . but what's wrong?"

"Would you mind to read my mother's letter? It's actually the second one of the three letters you gave me at the restaurant."

"Really! There were three letters inside that big envelope? Now . . . it makes more sense. If I understand you correctly; then there is another letter? So, have you read all three?"

"No, just the first two. Maybe you can read this one and help me understand it. Do you mind . . . it's fairly short?"

"Sure, but we'll leave after I read it . . . right?"

Handing him the letter, Kendra nodded before quietly answering, "Yes."

After quickly reading the letter, he handed it back before saying, "At least you'll be able to read the papers in a place where you'll feel comfortable and not in a hurry."

When he received no response, Timothy continued, "Honest to God, if I knew anything about any of this . . . mystery or whatever, I'd surely tell you. Let's head back and pick up your car. On a positive note, you're almost finished with the house."

"When you say almost, what do you mean? I thought I was finished with this awful place. You're not saying it will be necessary to come back . . . are you?"

Leaving the house and continuing to move slowly and carefully down the dirt trail, Timothy wanted to get his thoughts together before answering. Not looking in Kendra's direction, he eventually answered, "Finished with the physical part of seeing the house and checking out the contents of the attic—seemingly the most important part of this undertaking—but not its legal disposition."

Not fully grasping what he was saying, Kendra blurted out, "I don't want it. Do you think your father can help me understand what this is really all about? He must know something about the circumstances surrounding the house, and why Mother held on to it for all these years."

"I'm sure he does, but I don't know how much."

"But you'll ask him or help me talk to him . . . won't you?"

"Of course, I will. On the way to pick up your car, try to think of questions you may have. It's getting too late for us to get to Uvalde and find a notary. It's totally up to you, but I'd like you to stay in Uvalde, have a nice meal, and leave tomorrow for California. Again, it's your call, but I'm thinking you've put in a long and stressful day and should rest up before your trip back."

Without giving a direct answer or addressing any of Timothy's remarks, Kendra spoke softly, "I hope your father can help me."

Back on a better road to Sabinal—the worst of the roads finally behind them—Timothy watched Kendra close her eyes off and on—even dip her head a few times.

Patting the seat directly next to him, Timothy offered, "Better lay your head down before you fall over." To his surprise and without discussion, Kendra slid over next to him, placed her head against his shoulder, and was immediately asleep.

* * *

Tapping Kendra on the arm, Timothy said quietly, "Wake up Sleepy Head."

When he received no response, he said a tad louder, "Kendra, wake up. We're back at the restaurant parking lot."

Sitting up, blinking her eyes, and somewhat surprised, she replied, "That was fast."

Chuckling, Timothy answered, "Well, not really and not with any help from you. I'm not bragging, but I only made one wrong turn." Smiling, he continued, "I'm kidding with ya . . . you were exhausted."

"Sorry I flaked on you. Do you want to go inside and eat before we leave? It would be my treat this time."

Anticipating her question, Timothy answered quickly, "If you don't mind, I'd rather head to Uvalde and eat there,"

"Okay, you're right. There's no way I can leave tonight for California. How far is it to Uvalde from here?"

"About half an hour . . . give or take how traffic is flowing."

"That's not bad. So, when I follow you, where are we going to stop first," Kendra asked, wanting to plan her course of action in advance as well as her reply. She didn't look at the question as planning her agenda or making a timetable but rather knowing when she could cleanup . . . now uppermost on her mind.

"That's your call. Remember, I'm Sir Galahad and here to serve you."

Following a big yawn, Kendra asked, "And my choices would be?"

"I'm thinking: my office, finding you a hotel, and going to dinner."

"Are you talking about a hotel or motel?" she asked . . . thinking a hotel would be better.

"There's a nice hotel close to my office. I often have my out-of-town clients stay there and haven't received any complaints yet."

"Okay, then it's a done deal. I'd like to cleanup and change out of these dirty clothes. As far as your office goes, it sounds like we can't take care of anything tonight. Having said that, I want you to know how awful I feel about taking up so much of your time . . . like basically your entire weekend."

"I'd tell you if it was a problem. I've honestly enjoyed getting to know you. By the way, I forgot to ask if you're on a strict timeline to get back to California. You've given the appearance of being in a big rush to get home, so I want to work around your schedule. Again, I know it's a long way to California . . . probably a three day drive."

Here goes . . . she thought before answering. "Well, I have a month's leave-of-absence from my job." Wanting to quickly change the subject and avoid any discussion regarding her time off work, Kendra asked, "Does the hotel have a dining room?"

"Yes, but I've got a better idea. Let's skip the office and go directly to the hotel and get you registered. Then, I'll pick you up and take you to my favorite restaurant for dinner. How does that sound?"

"I'd like that . . . sounds perfect."

"Let me help you to your car, and then we'll be on our way to the big city of Uvalde."

Chapter 6

Following Timothy to Uvalde was easy and with his assistance, checking into the hotel was also easy. Her present dilemma—an especially difficult decision—was what outfit would be appropriate to wear to dinner. Her choice of attire was usually based on the destination, but in this particular case, the destination was unknown. As her therapist would say and has said many times before, "Pick out something you like and feel comfortable in and then go with it. Who cares, and you shouldn't."

Her additional problem and an important one . . . she had no idea whether or not Tim would care. Looking at the clock, she still had twenty-five minutes until he'd be there. Hmm, it was interesting to refer to him—off and on—as Tim instead of Timothy. Moving away from any silly thoughts . . . not connected with what to wear tonight, she opted for a comfortable—yet tasteful—outfit. Looking into the full-size mirror, she said out loud, "That should work."

Her only drawback in preparing to go out was the need to remove her contacts. She'd tried several times to clean them and use extra eye drops but nothing helped to ease her eyes from smarting. Wearing the contacts would not only be painful but her eyes would water throughout the meal. Appearing to cry during dinner would not be a pretty picture. Even though she didn't want Tim to see her with the thick ugly glasses on, she had no other choice but to wear them.

Answering the right-on-time knock at the door, Kendra was happy to see him but with mixed emotions. While feeling self-conscience because of her appearance change, she was impressed by his transformed appearance. He was wearing a sport coat and dress shirt, looking like an executive ready for a business meeting but purposely not wanting to overdress in a suit and tie. Wow, she thought, feeling drawn to him in an unknown strange way.

Even before saying, "Hello," Kendra said, "Sorry for the glasses switch."

"You're just fine. I considered wearing my glasses too, but my contacts weren't bothering me for a change," Timothy answered while smiling.

"Is what I'm wearing appropriate?" Kendra asked.

"Yes, absolutely, and you look very nice. But then, you always look nice to me."

That strange feeling returned with Tim's answer. Feeling embarrassed, she turned away for a moment . . . just in case her face was turning red. Recovering and appearing to check the room before leaving, she said, "Let me grab my purse. Oh, and before I forget, thank you again for moving the trunk into my car before you left earlier. No way could I have gotten through today without your help."

Kendra quit wondering, worrying, or even caring about where they'd be going to eat, deciding to enjoy her last day and forget about everything else. Tim stopped in front of a small—not at all a flashy or upscale looking—Italian restaurant. Trusting Tim's choice, she found it interesting that she was unable to remember the last time she'd eaten Italian food at an Italian restaurant.

When opening the car door, Tim offered with a big smile, "Getting in and out of my car will be a lot easier than from my daddy's pickup."

"It sure is," she answered with a similar big smile and took his hand.

Walking toward the entrance, Tim stated, "I hope you like Italian food."

After being seated, Kendra took a moment to casually look around the establishment. It had a comfortable feel to it. She couldn't keep from thinking how she'd never have the nerve before to try a new restaurant on her own. In fact, trying anything new had always been a struggle. Thinking the subtle Italian music—playing in the background—fit into the ambiance perfectly, and she began to relax. But when Tim asked if she had a favorite wine, she momentarily stuttered, "Ah . . . ah let me think a moment."

Before coming into the restaurant, Kendra had already decided not to give a single thought to calories or eating healthy. But what she hadn't considered was what she'd have to drink. She'd not had any alcohol since the episode with Albert and wasn't supposed to drink while on antidepressants.

Her answer following the short pause was, "I'm not much on drinking."

"Oh, I'm sorry. I'm sure they have lots of soft drinks, coffee, tea, and Texas sweet tea."

Patiently waiting for Tim to finish, she'd already changed her mind. "You know what; a glass of red wine sounds nice. You choose . . . more likely in your area of expertise than mine."

Instead of saying he wasn't a wine connoisseur, Timothy asked, "Do you mind if we order the wine and our meals at the same time. I don't want to rush you, but I'm starving."

"I bet you are, and I don't mind at all. I'm hungry too," Kendra quickly replied with a grin.

Grinning back, Timothy motioned for the server to come to their table. After receiving a carafe of house red wine and while waiting for their food, Tim toasted to their successful day. While sipping on their first glass, they made small talk about the town and the restaurant's history. Kendra learned that the original owner was a boyhood friend of Tim's father. After finishing her first glass, Kendra began to relax even more—perhaps due to the wine on an empty stomach—and was actually enjoying herself more than she thought possible.

After pouring each a second glass, Tim made another toast. "I want to wish you a safe trip home tomorrow." Although Kendra seemed relaxed and enjoying herself, he still needed to discuss the recent phone conversation he'd had with his daddy, especially since she'd be leaving the next day.

"So Kendra, I'm wondering if you've thought about any questions you may have?"

"No offense to you, but remember . . . I wanted to ask your father some questions."

"None taken but I did call my father to set that up. He said there was no rush on the house's disposition, saying he was not only your mother's attorney but also her friend through the years. He mentioned he'd had a long conversation with her just before receiving the envelope with the three letters. He also told me that he had no personal knowledge of the first two letters but did know what was in the third one . . . saying it was a copy of the trust. He assured your mother that the original trust was in his safe, and he'd explain everything to you . . . if necessary."

While Tim spoke, Kendra sat spellbound . . . not wanting to interrupt to ask questions for fear of disrupting his train of thought. Besides, she was learning some new information.

When he finally paused, Kendra inquired, "Did you tell him I had questions for him?"

"Yes, I did."

"Well, what was his answer?"

"Okay, I'll answer you with his exact words. 'Son, if I explained the trust, or the reasons for the stipulations, or what brought on the trust in the first place, it would be impossible for her to understand . . . at least at this point.

My suggestion for Kendra would be . . . first read the papers in the trunk. After that, she'll have a better understanding of the rest of it. Then, we can talk.'"

"That's it," Kendra answered with a frown.

"When I called to tell him you'd be giving him a call tonight or tomorrow, he told me he was just going to bed and would be getting up at dawn to go out on an all-day fishing trip."

"So . . . I'm leaving without answers," Kendra relied.

"Sorta, but on a positive note, you're getting closer."

"You sound just like my therapist," popped out before she could squelch the words. Never, ever did she volunteer personal information about her life. Damn it . . . now he'd wonder why she was seeing a therapist and want to know more.

Tilting his head questionably but not reacting directly to her therapist remark, Timothy asked, "Are you going to be okay?"

Wondering if Tim knew more than he'd let on, she asked, "What exactly do you mean?"

"Well, I was just wondering if you're going to be okay to wait for answers—relying on reading that mess of papers discovered in the trunk—instead of talking directly to my daddy?"

Feeling embarrassed because of overreacting, Kendra answered, "That makes sense."

The rest of the evening was full of light conversation. They talked about current events, food preferences, and Texas traditions. To Kendra, it felt like moving away from the trust, the house, and any negatives associated with them. If only for a short moment in time, she felt free of her current and necessary life decisions . . . but she liked—no loved—the new feelings.

On the way back to the hotel, Kendra began talking about things she'd never discussed with anyone besides her therapist. While blabbering on-and-on, she knew her loose lips were a direct result of the three glasses of wine but didn't care. "I feel I owe you an explanation for my sobbing when I saw the rose crumbling into pieces in the trunk. When I was in boarding school, it was a tradition to give your mother a single rose on Mother's Day. After I graduated, attended higher education, and even into adulthood, I continued the tradition. I knew the rose wasn't left for me, but as I watched it fall; it suddenly hit me . . . I could never give Mother a rose again. My sadness was also due in part to her never acknowledging my gift, and my never knowing why."

"Thank you for sharing that with me, and I want you to feel free to tell me anything." After saying that, he didn't pass on some interesting information his father had mentioned about her in confidence. Before their conversation ended, his father told him to be extra kind to Kendra.

When they arrived back at the hotel, Tim walked her to the room and even helped her with inserting the key card. She was actually giggling each time she missed the slot.

Standing in the partially opened door, Kendra said, "I'll be leaving early tomorrow so won't see you again. I want to thank you for the lovely dinner and for helping me with . . . well, with everything." Bravely said before gently bouncing against the door jam, she followed with, "I'm sincerely glad you came into my life if only for a short time. I will be forever grateful and never forget you."

As Timothy reached out to steady Kendra on the shoulder, many thoughts raced through his head like: having known Kendra for only a few days, remembering his daddy's words, and knowing it would be totally improper to kiss her. Yet, he still felt like they'd made a connection and wanted to kiss her goodbye anyway. Instead of following through on what he wanted to do, he asked, "Would you do me a favor by letting me know you've made it home safely? And Kendra, if you ever want to talk, please call me . . . okay?"

While thinking of giving him a hug or even better . . . a kiss, she knew a kiss would be improper, and she shouldn't . . . even in her state of whatever she was in. After all, she barely knew him. Instead, Kendra nodded her head yes before saying, "Goodbye Tim," and quickly closed the door before changing her mind.

Chapter 7

Before leaving Uvalde, Kendra made reservations to stay at the same places going home as she'd used coming to Sabinal. She didn't consider these repeated arrangements veering from being spontaneous, but rather using good judgment. She hoped her therapist would agree and consider her actions sensible.

Soon after arriving home and unpacking—separating the contents into piles of laundry and cleaning—she sat down and stared at the trunk . . . now resting in the middle of the living room. Kendra knew that once she opened the trunk and began reading through the hand-written papers, she'd be glued to the process until understanding what happened to her mother years ago. Hopefully, she'd also learn what her mother was unable to tell her.

Although exhausted from traveling and putting everything away, she needed—no wanted— to call Tim and let him know she'd gotten home safely. She needed to call—not only because she said she would—but also because it was the proper thing to do. Besides, following through with his request was the least she could do after everything he'd done for her. While listening to the phone ringing, she thought . . . why are you kidding yourself? You want to talk to him, so be honest with yourself. You miss the conversations, his advice . . . and him.

When his recorded message came on, she felt disappointed but left a message anyway, "Hi Tim . . . it's Kendra. Just wanted to let you know I made it home with no problems. I've been busy unpacking and planning to go to bed soon." Placing the phone down, Kendra asked herself . . . so why mention going to bed soon? Answering her own foolish question . . . because I can't wait to talk to him and want him to call me back soon, right away . . . even immediately.

Two hours later—while folding laundry—Tim returned her call. Not identifying himself, he offered, "Sorry, I was in court and unable to pick up. I didn't wake you . . . did I?"

"No, you didn't; I'm still trying to do catch-up on the necessary clean-up after traveling. While laughing, Kendra added, "Even though I've gained two hours, I'm still tired. I guess my inner clock and the different time zones aren't in sync yet."

"So, have you opened the trunk and tackled the contents yet," Tim asked hesitantly.

"Not yet, cuz I'm expecting it to be a full-time job, but I also know it needs to be done before going back to my real full-time job. I'm thinking the trunk housed the papers through the years so waiting a little longer shouldn't matter. Right?"

What Kendra didn't tell him was that she had an important appointment with her therapist the following day and knew it would be a long session. She had so much to tell her and so much to ask. Kendra had long ago realized that her therapist was not only the first person in her life to bounce ideas off of and receive suggestions from . . . but considered her to be her closest friend and confidant . . . like a parent should be.

While listening to Kendra discuss getting into the trunk to read the multitude of pieces of paper, Tim was thinking about having already read the trust. He knew and understood the "whats" but still wasn't sure about the "whys." He'd recognized the names involved but had questions regarding many of the stipulations. Bottom line, he hoped Kendra's therapist could help her as she ventured through the past and unraveled the secrets.

Knowing their conversation had paused uncomfortably, Tim answered quickly, "I think you're absolutely right . . . it has been years. You'll know when you're ready and the timing is right to open the trunk."

"If I get confused along the way, do you think your father can help me?" Kendra inquired.

"I'm sure he would but let me ask you a question. And before you answer, it will definitely be your call and totally up to you. Would you mind if I read the trust to possibly help you along the way? Keep in mind that the trust was facilitated and funded through my daddy's law firm—now also mine—and I'd always follow the rules of attorney-client privilege.

Kendra answered sincerely, "Tim, I trust you and have no problem with you reading the trust. However, I'm still going to follow your father's suggestion and delve into Mother's papers first. Would you please do me a big favor and let me know if you disagree with him . . . like in the next couple of days?"

Naturally relieved—since he'd already read the trust—Tim replied, "I will . . . absolutely."

"Sorry, but I need to get off the phone. I'm really getting sleepy and have no shoulder to lean on this time."

"That's an interesting concept; I should try that some time," Tim responded. When there was no answer, he thought maybe she'd already hung up. Just in case she was still on the phone, he offered, "You have a good night's rest and catch up."

"Thanks again for calling me back. I'll talk to you soon," Kendra answered with slurred words.

Tim responded with, "Sleep well . . . goodbye."

After Kendra replied, "Good night," and disconnected the call, the word "Good night" took her back to her college Literature Class and studying Shakespeare . . . remembering what Juliet said to Romeo, "Good night, good night. Parting is such sweet sorrow, that I shall say good night till it be morrow." If she'd said those words to Tim, would he have been impressed or thought she was weird? Well, it wouldn't be the first time to be considered weird, peculiar, odd, or introverted. Shaking her head, she felt too tired to add other names to the list.

As Kendra walked toward the bedroom, she started grinning. She could have said what Horatio said when he held Hamlet and watched him die, "Good night, sweet prince."

Once in bed and almost asleep, Kendra was glad she'd only said a simple good night.

* * *

Kendra's visit with her therapist went well. Her therapist was proud of her for addressing the Texas house head-on but was concerned about what she'd discover or not discover when she opened the trunk. Right before giving Kendra her private telephone number, she told her, "Try to control your expectations." Then she followed with, "You can contact me day or night if you need assistance."

When Kendra mentioned Tim and how he'd helped her, the therapist's response was similar to her answers in the past, "Take deep breaths, be thoughtful, and don't over-react with your emotions. You've come a long way, but right now you have a lot on your shoulders, and your emotions are raw. Plus, you're still dealing with the social media fiasco, and your mother's death."

Chapter 8

Once the trunk's lid was up—hoping it wasn't as bad as remembered—Kendra took a deep breath and looked inside. It smelled awful, and Tim was right; it was a mess at the Texas house and still was . . . maybe it was worse after moving the trunk around.

While driving home, Kendra constantly thought about the best way to organize the papers . . . deciding to stack them according to their dates. Without a starting date or the timing between the first and last one, her strategy would be to concentrate only on the dates instead of reading them out of order. Even at best, she assumed the papers would be difficult to piece together and hard to understand.

As she peered below at the intertwined papers—and if she was right—the oldest would be at the bottom—face-up—and the later ones placed toward the top Baffled by how to proceed, she thought about calling Tim to see if he had a suggestion. Instead, she told herself to figure it out on her own. After all, she'd come a long way on decision making . . . even her therapist said so.

Determined not to read anything and just look for dates, Kendra began to carefully dig into the trunk. To make matters worse, most were face-up, while others were scattered pointing downward. She tried to keep the few undated slips of papers above and below where they originally rested. Since not stacked directly on top of each other and randomly added to the trunk, it was difficult and almost impossible to do. Leaning over the trunk was becoming uncomfortable . . . beginning to feel an off-and-on dull ache in her lower back.

After the first hour passed with little progress, the thought crossed her mind of dumping the entire trunk up-side-down but decided that would surely make it worse—mixing up the dates even more. Okay . . . new plan. I'll move groups—clutching a section from top to bottom—and place them up-side-down in separate stacks around the dining room table. If thinking correctly, this would put the oldest on top. Whether a good, bad, or indifferent idea, it took a good half hour to empty the trunk. When finished, the rose pieces—having filtered to the bottom—remained alone, causing her to feel sad but not like before.

Trying not to look at the words, Kendra concentrated on locating a date on each piece of paper. It was taking hours to sort through the different sizes and shapes. Oddly enough, the oldest ones were mostly on the same form . . . usually written on both sides of restaurant guest checks. There were a few with brief orders on them like: 1 cof/ blk, or 1 7-up/no ice, or 1 choc muf. She thought how interesting it would be to know what items cost back then and was disappointed when no prices were listed.

While paying close attention to the dates, Kendra noticed the early guest checks were mostly in numerical order, helping to make the date search somewhat easier. It seemed as if they were torn from a pad and purposely used to write on. Without reading them—hard to do since being so curious—she again noticed the writing on both sides . . . using the dated side to read first.

Once when looking for a date, the name "San Antonio" caught her attention . . . reminding her of asking her mother about being born in San Antonio—clearly on her birth certificate—but Mother's answer was always vague. "Because that's where I was when I gave birth to you." When she'd asked why in San Antonio, there was never a reply. So, through the years, she'd quit asking . . . tired of being ignored or hearing Mother's favorite answer, "It's none of your concern."

Kendra finally found what she thought was the first slip of paper added to the trunk. It had a partial date on it—Sept ? 1989. What did the question mark mean? Did her mother not know the date or what? How could that be? Finding the year interesting—since she was born in 1992—she could somewhat place a timeline prior to her birth. Afraid she might forget important dates, Kendra looked for a notebook pad to jot down what might become important for her to read later or find on the computer.

When finally stopping, Kendra didn't think the dates were perfect but felt too tired to double check them. Since her entire day had been devoted to organizing, she decided to stop and begin again tomorrow.

Realizing she hadn't eaten all day, she went to the kitchen to find something that sounded good. Remembering she'd cleaned the refrigerator out before leaving for Texas, she had meant to go grocery shopping today. Wondering what was available, she thought about cereal but had no milk so decided to grab a slice of frozen bread, put it in the toaster, and cover it with peanut butter. Unable to wash it down with a glass of milk, she made a cup of tea.

The following morning, Kendra went to the grocery store first . . . being afraid of getting involved and ending up like the day before. She could hardly wait to have a bowl of granola cereal with sliced bananas. Then, wondered if she'd gained weight while traveling. Oh well, she'd worry about that later. Right now, she was more curious about reading her mother's notes.

It was all so confusing. Some of the oldest guest checks were labeled Bob's Bus Stop Café. She almost stopped to see if the cafe could be found on her computer, where it was located, or if it still existed. No . . . not right now, that could wait. However, she did add it to the list of questions and dates to check on later.

Reading through her mother's notes, Kendra tried to visualize how she looked back then. Since she'd never seen any pictures of her mother when young, it was impossible to do. Even now, the only pictures she had of Mother were the ones she'd taken, starting with the cell phone she'd received on her twelfth birthday. How strange— even complicated—this all seems, she thought. Through the years, she'd never actually known her mother's birth date until seeing it on her death certificate. Although her mother had told her the day and the month, she'd never volunteered the year. It became another question asked with a "none of your concern answer." If possible, the complicated was getting more complicated, Kendra thought. Also . . . the whys. Before I go any further and afraid of forgetting a place, a date, a name, or something deemed important, she needed to add anything suspicious, unknown, or questionable to the notebook. The list was already becoming long, and she'd only just begun.

Adding her mother's birthday to the growing list—next to the date of the first writing—and if calculating correctly, her mother would have been seventeen years old then. So, was her mother a waitress at Bob's Bus Stop Café when she wrote on those guest checks? Did she possibly find the order slips and not actually work there? Trying to keep an open mind at this point, she really wasn't certain of anything. However, one thing was for certain—even though barely starting—she'd already learned some interesting information and couldn't wait to discover more.

If she wasn't on leave from work, she could have added the dates into a data sheet, and the information would be processed and organized within seconds. It was her first time to think of work—other than mentioning her time off to Tim. Although she liked the solitude of plugging in statistics and not interacting with others, she had become—even enjoying—being in new social situations . . . especially with Tim.

As she progressed through the days of her mother's life—instead of concentrating on each word by itself—Kendra tried to put the words into story form. One thing that stood out on a few of the early guest checks were the initials C B. Why not C S? She'd add both sets of initials to her notebook.

Some of the written entries were more detailed than others. Some were written on both sides of large pieces of paper . . . like her mother had more time to write. Reading them became a long and tedious process but was also fascinating. Sometimes, the words were difficult to decipher—almost scribbled—and she often needed to read them several times to grasp their meaning.

When reading one fairly long and detailed sheet, she became shocked beyond words.

I don't know if I'm safe or not. He's looking for me. I'm not that far away. Today I found a missing persons flier on the post outside. Took it down. I've changed my looks by cutting my hair and will dye it when I get $. Changed my last name to Smith. That's a pretty common name. I'm going to keep a diary like I did at home but left it behind when I left in a hurry. I'm going to write stuff down about why I ran away just in case something happens to me. I must remember to call myself Chris Smith instead of Christine Brooks. It's hard to change. Guess I'll learn.

Christine's Story
(as gleaned from her notes)

Graduating from Uvalde High School—first in my class—was very exciting. It was the happiest day of my life. It meant I could leave home and go to college in San Antonio. The best part of graduating; I'd be free from my abusive step-father and his drunkenness. My two older brothers had already escaped, finding jobs in other parts of Texas. I only heard from them once, saying they were okay and didn't want him to know where they were. They asked me to tell Mom they were happy and okay. Tell Mom not to worry.

I always wondered why my mom put up with his drinking and meanness. She said staying was what she had to do. What could a woman do with no skills and three children to raise up? It was hard enough to get by with her husband's frequent lost jobs, fighting at the bars, and a couple of trips to jail. There were no secrets in our house. We heard and knew everything. We kids stayed away as much as possible. My brothers were big into sports, and I spent most of my time studying at the library. I wanted to make good grades, so I could go to college.

The last straw before deciding to run away was when my step-father said I couldn't leave to go to college. I had to stay and find a job in Uvalde to help support the family. He'd just been fired for drinking on the job—per Mom— but he said he was laid off.

My lifelong ambitions were to write—especially poetry—get married, and have a family.

College was my only hope for a good future. I knew if I didn't leave as soon as possible; I never could. I began saving money from baby-sitting which wasn't much. Thinking I'd have enough put away in about a month, but my step-father suddenly demanded all the money I'd saved.

He pushed me around and threw me out of my bedroom. Thank goodness, I hid the money in several places, so he didn't find all of it. As soon as he passed-out, I gathered what little money he didn't find, grabbed a few articles of clothing, and ran to the bus stop.

When I asked for a ticket to San Antonio, I didn't have enough money so asked for a ticket to take me as far as I could go. That happened to be Sabinal. Disappointed and almost in tears, I was determined to find a job in Sabinal and make enough to go on to San Antonio. One way or another, or like Scarlett said in *Gone with the Wind,* "As God is my witness, they're not going to lick me. I'm going to live through this and when it's all over, I'll never be hungry again." In my case I didn't care if I'd be hungry, but my step-father wouldn't lick me from going to college.

When the bus stopped in front of Bob's Bus Stop Café, I wondered how far from Uvalde I'd traveled, and how far I was from San Antonio? I'd heard of Sabinal before, but never been out of the town of Uvalde. But then, I'd only lived in Uvalde for two years . . . two school years. That was about the same amount of time as we stayed anywhere. I tried to look grown-up . . . like I was right where I wanted to be. I carried my small beat-up suitcase inside and sat at a booth near the doorway to the restroom sign . . . just in case I needed to hide. Nervous about what I'd ask for; I sat and waited at that empty booth in that empty room.

Finally, a man came from somewhere in the back and asked, "What can I get for you, Honey? I hopes you're not waiting for the bus, cuz it already left."

Without replying to the bus remark and too embarrassed to tell him I only had a little money—less than a dollar—I asked, "Could I just have a glass of water?"

"Yes ma'am. Will ya be waiting for the next bus, cuz it ain't coming 'til lots later?"

"No sir . . . I'm just resting for a bit. I'm looking for a job . . . trying to save enough money, 'til I can travel on to San Antonio."

"Well, I declare. Can you wait tables? My help left yesterday to have her baby. It's slow around these parts.

I do the cooking but travelers don't eat much . . . mostly have a drink or two waiting for the bus."

* * *

Kendra was fascinated beyond words . . . savoring the writings on each and every slip of paper. Such a treasure trove of information she was learning. As she progressed through the dated notes—entered daily and sometimes more often—the first page of her own notebook was bursting with questions and dates. She debated on whether to stop and look up her entered questions or wait until further along into her mother's life. Thinking it was a no-brainer; it seemed better to stop reading now and find answers . . . as that would definitely help her have a better understanding into her mother's scribblings. Opting to follow up on the notebook entries—while fresh on her mind—Kendra stepped away from the dining room table.

Stretching and yawning, she smiled while thinking of what Scarlett said at the end of *Gone with the Wind*, "After all, tomorrow is another day."

Although tired, Kendra wanted to do some research on her computer—checking out Uvalde's and Sabinal's history—learning Bob's Bus Stop Café had been closed for years. Once the bus route moved across town, Bob's Bus Stop Café was doomed and closed permanently in 1997. Researching more, it had changed hands many times from a bus stop to several small beer bars.

Chapter 9

Waking early and feeling refreshed—the first time since returning from Texas—Kendra mixed together a vegetarian omelet. While eating her breakfast—full of yummy broccoli—she kept thinking of the different meals she'd had with Tim and wishing he'd call her. Deciding to take a much needed walk, Kendra continued to think of Tim and remembered how safe she'd felt when placing her head on his shoulder and falling asleep. Even the possibility of Tim having a single thought about her in return bordered on silliness. However and regardless, she still couldn't keep from wondering if he ever thought of her. When these silly thoughts surfaced, she reminded herself that perhaps he was just being a helpful person. But in spite of these frequent thoughts of his sense of humor and kind gestures, there still remained the possibility that his generous acts were carried out for financial gain. Either way or whatever, she missed him.

Returning from her brief walk, Kendra took a quick shower, fixed a juice drink, put on comfortable lounging pajamas, and sat down at the dining room table . . . ready to tackle the slightly reduced stacks before her. As she picked up the next dated piece of paper, her anticipation level was already on high-alert for new information . . . good, bad, or indifferent.

* * *

I was sure happy when Bob offered me a job. Even better—because I was too embarrassed to ask him—he said he needed me to help him out. I had no idea what I was doing, but Bob was real patient with me. It didn't take long to learn how to abbreviate the orders. Bob would laugh and say, "Honey, people are hankerin' for their grub. They ain't got time for your story-writin' on their bill. I'll get the gist of it. If not, I know where to find ya." Every day, I find myself wishing Bob could have been my father.

I'm thinking; it makes no-never-mind to know who or where my real father is or was. For sure . . . anyone would be better than my step-father.

I'm glad we don't have much business while I'm learning what to do, It gives me lots of time to write in my diary. I'm doing the best I can to find paper to write on. I'm sure Bob wishes we had lots more customers, but he tells me he likes helping me learn. Bob says I'm a fast learner and move a lot faster than Bessie did. Then, he'll laugh and say, "Well, Bessie was carrying a mighty big load around." We play cards and dominos when it's extra slow.

With my first pay—which wasn't much after a small deduction for the room—I was able to buy a few needed items from the second-hand store but couldn't find paper or a notebook. Bob doesn't charge me for vittles. He says it's fair, cuz I eat like a bird. He also never asks any questions about my reasons for being here or about my plans when I get to San Antonio. I never tell him anything about me or my past. I'm getting better at saying my first name is Chris.

After almost a month, I'm half-way to saving enough for my ticket to San Antonio. Bessie had her baby but is having a difficult time with her recovery. She asked Bob for another month off. I was relieved when he told her, "No worries cuz we're doing just fine. You take care of yourself and the little one . . . you hear." I wanted to ask Bob if he had any family but decided that could open a can of worms. My step-father said, "Can of worms" all the time. Then that reminded me of catching mice to feed his snake. Oh dear, just thinking of him makes me sick.

Knowing I'll be off to San Antonio soon, I'm starting to relax and feel a bit safer. My life isn't great but compared to living at home . . . it's wonderful.

It was a slower than usual Wednesday afternoon when my life changed . . . like really changed. Bob and I were playing cards—five-card draw—and for the first time, I was way ahead. I had a big pile of toothpicks in front of me and couldn't keep from giggling with each win. I'm getting real good at bluffing and think Bob is both surprised and pleased . . . as in, I'm a good teacher at cards too. Well,

I'll never forget that day. That's when a ranch hand named Chuck strolled into Bob's Bus Stop Café and into my life. His snakeskin boots were the first thing I noticed . . . even before he said with a big smile, "Howdy . . . I'm Chuck."

Chuck looked years younger than Bob but lots older than me. Without being invited, he sat down in the booth next to Bob before asking, "Can you deal me in?"

Bob hesitantly inquired, "How you fixed for toothpicks?"

"I reckon . . . I'm busted," was said before asking with a grin, "How about a couple of hands on the house . . . say toothpick credit?"

I didn't say anything, just handed him a few toothpicks from my stack. After he lost three hands, he offered a toothpick back before saying, "Too high-stakes for me. Here's one toothpick back, and I owe you." With a smile and a wink, he then asked, "Darlin', what's your name?"

"It's Chris."

"Well, Chris . . . do you have a last name?" he asked with another big smile.

"It's Smith," I answered, trying to seem like I was telling the truth.

"Well, you sure look familiar to me. Have we met before?"

"No sir," I answered.

"Well . . . Miss, I hope to make you acquaintance again real soon."

After he left, I asked Bob if he'd seen him before. Bob shook his head but told me he must be living in high cotton, cuz them boots he had on were mighty expensive. We agreed it was odd for him to stop in and not ask for a bus schedule or want something to eat or drink.

A few days later, Chuck came back in, nodded to me, and asked to talk to Bob. I heard Bob say, "It's none of anyone's business . . . leave her be."

I had the sinking feeling they were talking about me. Their conversation was interrupted when a couple with two children came inside. They said they'd sit a spell and eat while waiting for the next bus. After giving them water and taking their orders, I asked Bob what Chuck wanted. Bob told me that we'd talk later after he fixed three burgers . . . reminding me to split the one burger between the two kids. After the family was on the bus, the table cleared, and the floor swept below where the messy kids sat, Bob said, "Let's sit a spell. We need to talk."

Bob didn't seem surprised when he offered, "That guy, Chuck, recognized your picture from a missing person's flyer."

I began to cry and told Bob everything . . . all my reasons for running away from home. I explained how my mean and drunken step-father refused to let me go to college in San Antonio . . . telling me I could never leave. Sobbing, I asked if he'd loan me enough money to get me to San Antonio. Before he had a chance to answer, I promised to pay him back. "Honey, you know I would, but Chuck says the posters are all over the bus station in San Antonio and even some still around Sabinal. I'm sorry . . . I's thinking the ones here abouts were gone."

I blurted out a bunch of questions like: "Did you already know? Where can I go? Do you think Chuck's telling the truth?" Then, I finally pleaded, "Bob, what I should do?"

When Bob didn't answer and ducked his head, I ran to my room and started gathering my things. I didn't know where I was going or what to do, but—no matter what happened—I'd never go back. I couldn't quit crying and wanted to get under the bed and hide. Only a few months away from turning eighteen, surely I'd be considered an adult after my birthday. Could the authorities make me go back then?

When I heard a knock at my door, I told Bob to go away. When the knocking continued, Bob said, "Chuck is downstairs and wants to talk to you. I think you should hear him out."

Between sobs, I asked Bob if he'd brought the Texas Rangers with him.

Bob answered quickly, "No, he's alone . . . says he may have an answer to your predicament."

After grabbing a tissue and blowing my nose, I slowly opened the door. I asked Bob if he'd go downstairs and help me talk to Chuck. Bob answered seriously, "No Honey, this has got to be your decision . . . only yours, but I'll be close by."

Even before sitting down, Chuck began. "I wish you no harm, but I'm thinking you are in a world of hurt. Bob told me why you left home. I'm thinking you need help, and I've got an idea. On the ranch where I work, there's a vacant house. You or Bob can verify that I work there, and that the old house exists. I'm thinking you could stay there until things cool off and people are no longer looking for you. The owner of the ranch lets the ranch hands stay there now and then . . . especially when the cattle are being moved to a near-by section of land. The house only has a few basics, but I'd be willing to help you with vittles."

"Why do you want to help me? Won't you get in trouble?" I asked.

"No, cuz I've just been moved up to foreman. The house is a far piece from town, and I'm thinking the ranch company pays no-never-mind to it being there. Besides, the company owners mostly live in Dallas and Austin." Chuck then proudly offered, "See these here boots, purchased them with my savings and new pay hike."

"Are you sure you won't get into trouble?" I asked again.

"No ma'am. I ain't worried about it. It's only for a short spell until no one's looking for ya."

"I can't pay rent or nothing to you," I told him straight out.

"I understand. That's not what I'm saying. I don't want anything from you . . . just trying to help you out of a tough spot."

"Do you know if a person is eighteen; can they make them go back if caught?"

"I can't rightly say . . . but I'm thinking . . . most likely not."

"Even though I don't have much choice right now, I'd kinda like to know what my druthers are before making a final decision. I'm thinking maybe Bob can find out.,"

"I'll also ask around, but I've got to be careful with any questions. The Rangers get suspicious when you ask too many questions. Then, they start asking questions back . . . if you get my drift. I hear they're looking close to the towns around Uvalde again. They might even show up here real soon."

"Thank you for offering but I want to talk to Bob. Could I get your phone number?"

"No, I'm not in one place long enough to have one . . . mostly staying in a ranch barn outside where the herds are grazing. Don't take too long to make up your mind. I'd like to help you before it's too late. If they're stepping up their search, someone will surely recognize you . . . like I did."

"Oh dear, I can't go back there. I'd rather die first."

"Now . . . now Honey. Please don't fret. I'll carry you to safe place . . . promise. I'll be back tomorrow to fetch you."

When I talked to Bob, he didn't think it was a good idea. "We know nothing about this Chuck guy. We don't even know his last name." I argued that I didn't have another choice, and it would only be for a short time. Bob said things like: "I have no way to contact you or him. I have no idea where you'll be going. What if he's a bad guy and means harm to ya?"

I assured Bob that I'd keep in touch some way. I'd make Chuck promise to check-in with him . . . at least until I turned eighteen. I pleaded with Bob to find out if they could make me go back home once I was eighteen. I continued to assure Bob that Chuck only wanted to help me and seemed like a good person. At this point, nothing Bob could say would change my mind. I finally told him, "I'd rather die trying to be safe than going back with my step-father."

"Okay, little lady, I do know that a person who knowingly helps a run-away can be charged with kidnapping . . . even if the run-away says differently. I know that because my cousin went to jail for that years ago. I'm just saying."

Bob said he'd give me the metal trunk—located below the window in my room—to use. He said it was empty and hadn't been used in years. I was glad, cuz no way could the small suitcase I'd brought hold what I'd gathered since living there. I rushed to throw clothes into the trunk before Bob noticed I'd already been using it—without permission—to place my diary papers in. Bob reluctantly tried to lend a hand but finally walked to the door. Right before leaving, he turned and said, "I'm going to worry about you every day. Even though we've only known each other for a short time, I've come to think of you like the daughter I never had. Please let me know how you're doing."

I don't think of myself as a religious person, but tonight I'll pray that I'm making the right decision.

This morning, after I finished gathering the last of my meager possessions, I sat down on the bed, looked around the room, and prayed again. Finally, I told myself that if leaving isn't a good idea, I'd somehow get back to Bob's Café and Bob. Even though Chuck said he'd keep me safe, I knew—for sure—I'd been safe with Bob . . . at least so far.

Smiling, Chuck arrived early to pick me up. Just before getting into his old pick-up truck, Bob whispered,

"Somehow keep in touch and be careful. I'll be waiting to hear from ya."

The trip to my unknown destination was dreadful. The roads were full of deep holes and sometimes the roads completely disappeared. We traveled farther than I'd imagined possible. It seemed like it took forever but maybe felt that way cuz of the slow going. I found myself trying to memorize how to get back to Sabinal—if I needed to or wanted to—but gave up and did my best to hang on for dear life to the truck's seat.

Finally, the house appeared out of nowhere. It was all by itself with nothing around it . . . not even a single tree. I was happily surprised, because it looked like a nice house . . . small but had a big front porch. Without going inside and with my first look, it already seemed better than any of the rental houses I'd lived in before. I don't know how to exactly describe it, but it sure looks deserted . . . like no one's lived there in a long time.

Chuck carried the trunk in first before going back to fetch a couple of sacks of food. While he was doing that, I briefly wandered through the house. There is some furniture in the house like: a sofa and a couple of chairs in the living room, a small kitchen table with two chairs, and one bedroom with a bed and chest of drawers. I wondered if the old refrigerator worked but didn't want Chuck to catch me being nosey.

It is very quiet here. I can't hear a single sound from either inside or outside the house. Usually birds are chirping in the countryside but only silence is everywhere here abouts. I feel like crying but better not. And even though I'm scared, I don't want to look like I'm frightened to Chuck. Although I'm afraid now, I know it will be a lot worse when Chuck leaves . . . and I'm alone. Maybe I should ask Chuck to take me back to Sabinal? No, I've got to stay and be brave. I keep telling myself . . . girl, get ahold of yourself and be brave; get ahold of yourself and you'll be okay.

When Chuck came inside and placed the two big sacks of groceries on the table, he offered, "I know the place isn't much, but no one can ever find you out here."

Chapter 10

Kendra stopped reading and pushed back from the table. Gazing at the clock, it was surprising to see it was an hour past her usual lunch time. Wondering what sounded good to eat, she realized she really wasn't hungry . . . having a strange feeling of doom settling over her. Although curious and wanting to read more, she was concerned about what could or would happen to her mother after Chuck's remark of "no one ever finding her."

She wished the process of reading the papers was easier, wanting to move along at a quicker pace. Trying to understand the mismatched pieces of papers with small scribbled words was tedious at best. Although she could empathize with her mother fleeing from the area, it also felt similar to reading a scary book . . . waiting for something unforeseen or dangerous to happen.

Sighing with a hushed groan, Kendra reminded herself that Mother had clearly made it to California from Texas. However, the why, when, and even how were still unknown. Since she'd been born in San Antonio, the questions also applied to her. Chastising herself for having concerns about something that happened long ago and couldn't be changed, she should try to remove herself from any personal connections while reading. Tomorrow, she had another appointment with her therapist and needed to concentrate on her own forward progress . . . right now in the present.

Taking a break from reading and the accompanying eye strain, Kendra walked to the bathroom to put drops in her eyes. While blinking several times, her episode with Albert surfaced again. Since acquiring the contacts had been her first act of becoming a new person—after the encounter with Albert—Kendra couldn't help but wonder if her contacts would always remind her of that dreadful time. Then she wondered if her therapist considered her actions with Albert just as bazaar as she considered what her mother was doing in the wilderness with Chuck. Well, she'd survived Albert and was better at addressing new circumstances . . . and her mother must have also survived . . . whatever she'd faced back then. Perhaps she'd learn that Chuck's motives were totally different from Albert's, were on the up-and-up, and her uneasy feelings were unwarranted. Surely time and more reading would let her know. If nothing else . . . she needed to quit wondering and focus on her mother's actual words.

Soon after administering the eye drops and still not hungry, Kendra decided to lie down, relax, and rest her eyes. She stretched out on the bed and closed her eyes. Taking care of her eyes and addressing her contacts sent her back again to meeting Albert and his first remark. "You're not as ugly as I thought you were," he'd said matter-of-factly. He quickly followed with, "Do you really need to wear those thick glasses?" She'd not answered . . . remembering their meeting as if it happened yesterday. She'd not replied because he was just telling the truth; she was ugly. Besides, it hadn't been the first time to be considered ugly . . . having been called ugly when young and unattractive when older.

Through the years, Mother told her—no, preached— to stay away from the opposite sex, constantly stressing how they were only after sex and couldn't be trusted. "Don't gussie yourself up to attract them . . . nothing good can come of it." It was difficult to remember exactly when Mother started stressing the evils of being noticed . . . maybe before boarding school. That would put her back to at least the fifth grade. She also couldn't remember when she wasn't told how to dress, how to act, how to wear her hair—parted in the middle and straight down— and to never-ever use make-up. "It might attract the wrong person," was constantly stressed. Never knowing who the wrong person could or would be, she'd tried to stay away from everyone.

According to her therapist, Mother's actions bordered on a form of child abuse and probably—most likely—led to the dire consequences with Albert. But regardless of how the therapist viewed Mother, she could never blame her. She just couldn't. Perhaps she'd been naïve but assumed mothers were supposed to protect their children from harm. Mother's actions seemed perfectly normal back then . . . just making sure that no one took advantage of her daughter. Growing up, it was an accepted part of her life. When reading more of her mother's story, she'd hopefully learn why her mother behaved and spoke the way she did.

When she turned twenty-six, Mother told her, "Kendra, I can no longer afford to take care of you. You've got to move out and take care of yourself."

After the initial shock and not understanding the reason, she'd asked a simple, "Why?"

Mother's answer was different from her usual reply of, "Not your concern." This time the answer was more direct, "That's the way it is . . . no discussion. Now you can deal with it."

Moving out on her own—abruptly truly alone—her life functioned just fine. Actually, her life became better than fine. She no longer had to manage her life—twenty-four seven—according to her mother's wishes. She was still leading the same quiet life—not bothering anyone—and no one ever reached out to interact with her. But then, she'd always been more or less alone . . . generally away at numerous boarding schools, college, and grad school. Even after moving out, Mother continued to say, "Kendra, you'll always be indebted to me for your expensive education, for your car, for your insurances," and on-and-on . . . even for your life. "I could have gotten rid of you but chose not to," she'd offered many times. Soon after moving out, the telephone conversations with her mother became less and less . . . then almost stopped.

By that time, she was already making a decent salary—working for a data processing firm—and had no problem paying her own bills and necessary expenses. She was finally self-sufficient; which meant she no longer needed to ask or discuss money with her mother. Her life was very basic. Each day, she went to work in her designated cubby-hole and clicked in figures all day . . . spending hours on formatting or transforming output and conversions of raw data. Sometimes, when watching others laughing and enjoying each other's company, she'd momentarily wonder why she didn't have acquaintances like her co-workers had—let alone friends—but in reality it never felt like she was missing out on anything.

After work, she'd usually go directly back to her apartment. Even so, it was difficult to escape Mother's past words of indoctrination, "Never let anyone get close; they'll always hurt you. If not right away, it will eventually happen."

Albert didn't come to pass until she turned twenty-eight . . . just a mere two years ago. However, sometimes it still felt like yesterday.

One night, while working on a general application problem at home, a note popped up on her computer. "Want to escape from your boring life of data processing? I'm here for you." What the heck! Smiling, she'd thought . . . is Big Brother watching me? Continuing on with the complicated but interesting data research, a similar message said, "I do data processing too and need someone to talk to. Won't you talk to me?" Then, another message followed in bold letters. **"Do you want . . . to talk . . . to a like-minded person?"** The choppy wording reminded her of how a robot would speak.

So, why not answer; she questioned. After all, she had a great virus protection system on her computer. What could it hurt?

Chapter 11

Once the back-and-forth started with Albert, Kendra was hooked. She'd never paid attention to social pop-ups . . . but then, none had ever referenced data processing before. During their initial conversations, the challenges of data gathering were enthusiastically discussed and how others considered it boring. It was intriguing to find another person who understood the difficult process and stress of number crunching.

From the very beginning, they agreed on everything. It was her first time to discuss—outside of college classes and during the hiring interviews—the importance of helping businesses rely on data numbers to achieve advantages over their competitors. It was also her first time to receive praise and compliments for her professional insights and for the difficult work she performed. "You are absolutely terrific," and "How lucky that I found you," and Albert's most common compliment, "I love talking to you."

After a couple of weeks of sharing business interests, Albert began to talk about personal likes and dislikes. Again, he was agreeable to anything discussed during these conversations . . . constantly complementing her on anything she said or mentioned. Soon, Kendra began to think of Albert as her very first friend and looked forward to his phone calls.

When Albert began to push to see her in person—maybe three weeks had passed—Kendra held back for many reasons but mostly wanting to continue talking anonymously without judgment about her looks, how she dressed, or any of her life-long insecurities.

As she often did when it was quiet . . . thoughts of how stupid she'd been not to question Albert about how he found her, or how he knew she was a data processer.

Now able to see the situation with Albert objectively, she really wished she'd been talking to a therapist during that time. Without a doubt, she'd been more careful—not only more careful about meeting Albert—but more aware of what he was doing to draw her into his world of deceit. Another no-brainer . . . guidance and suggestions from a therapist would have protected her from a whole lot of pain and suffering.

Returning her thoughts to the present and her therapist's statements at their last session, "Kendra, you need to concentrate on letting go of the past. Be proud of the forward progress you've made. Right now—in the present—you should celebrate the self-awareness you currently possess."

Knowing her therapist was right, she'd spent way too much time on the past in general and on the mishap with Albert in particular. It was becoming easier and easier to look at her past as a learning experience. It was also becoming easier and easier not to cry. And above all, it was becoming easier and easier to distance herself from the returning thoughts of self- recriminations.

Feeling ready to tackle her mother's notes again, Kendra returned to the dining room table.

* * *

Chris watched Chuck leave and quickly returned inside. Not nearly as afraid as she thought she'd be; she wandered through the house, trying to picture what the people who'd lived there were like, and why they'd left. As she checked out each room more carefully, Kendra continued to speculate on why the house had been built so far out from civilization in the first place . . . miles from other houses or buildings. She could understand using the house later on for cattle workers—according to Chuck— but didn't understand not seeing cattle grazing on the trip out there or close by. Reconsidering, perhaps the cattle were sold or moved elsewhere long ago and the occupants followed. When Chuck returned, she'd try to remember to ask him about the circumstances surrounding the house. On second thought, the house's history of who, why, or when really didn't matter, cuz she'd just be staying there for only a short time before leaving for San Antonio to go to school.

The daily short walks outside the house didn't help much to pass the time and neither did the longer walks farther out. The only thing that somewhat kept her from worrying about Chuck returning was the time she was spending on writing down her innermost thoughts in her diary. Frowning, how could she call the gathered scraps of misshapen papers her diary? Turning the frown into a smile, perhaps when she enrolled in college, she could take a literature class and write a short story about her adventures of staying in an abandoned house in the middle of Texas.

Although Chuck hadn't said exactly when he'd return, he did say he'd be back soon. Trying to keep track of the days could become a problem. At the moment, she knew she'd been waiting for him for three days but knew—as the days went along—the days could blend together. Wishing she'd thought to bring a calendar; she didn't even have a watch or a clock. It was already becoming an odd way of life . . . without scheduling each day according to things to do and when they needed to be accomplished. She remembered seeing a movie where a prisoner put marks on the wall to count the days and began to shiver. While knowing she certainly wasn't a prisoner, she did feel alone and isolated. It was reassuring that she'd been diligent about dating her diary notes and making sure to carefully place them on top of the others in Bob's trunk.

Not planning to stay long, Kendra was especially grateful that the plumbing and electricity were working. She hadn't expected any frills but could use a few items to make her short time there a bit better. Realizing she hadn't thought about necessities—except for food—she began to make a list: washing soap to clean clothes in the tub, at least two towels and wash cloths, and especially toilet paper. The roll of paper towels on top of the toilet tank was gross.

Since Chuck was adamant for her to stay in the truck while he went into the grocery store to shop; perhaps he wouldn't mind to gather a few more needed items for her. Was he being especially nice to go in and pay for the groceries or was he afraid to be caught with a runaway?

Once the list was completed, she'd write a note to Bob, so he'd know she was okay. Should she impose on Chuck to deliver the note or ask for stamps and an envelope? So many questions to ask and so many items needed . . . noting the list was growing as each day turned into another. Each time she added something to the list, she wondered why Chuck was being so nice and generous. In her entire life—besides Bob—Chuck was the only man to ever be kind to her.

She had just taken her first bite of a fried hamburger patty on white bread when hearing the sound of tires drawing near. Running excitedly to the window, she was confused by a different pickup approaching . . . and afraid. Should she hide? Had someone found her?

It was at the end of the fifth day and almost dark outside when a light blue pickup drove up slowly in front of the house. As it carefully backed up to park—facing the opposite direction—her eyes fixated on the huge longhorns attached to the truck's front hood. She quickly moved the dusty curtains aside for a better look. Feeling her heart pounding, she waited to see who would get out of the truck. Thoughts rushed through her head like: who was there, did they know she was inside the house, should she run out the back door but then . . . where could she hide? To her amazement and relief, Chuck stepped out from the driver's side.

She carefully watched as he went to the back of the truck and began unloading several large boxes and a few smaller ones. Unable to contain herself any longer, she unlocked the front door and literally ran outside and jumped down the front steps. Once close to him, she unexpectedly jumped into his arms, momentarily clinging onto him.

"Now . . . that's the kind of welcome a guy likes to receive," Chuck said with a chuckle.

Beyond embarrassed, she quickly answered, "I was afraid you'd forgotten me."

"Surely you didn't really worry about that," he replied with a frown.

Feeling a tad silly and not acting grown up, she said, "Well, it is very deserted out here."

"So, you missed me. Is that what you're saying?"

"Yes Sir," she answered quickly.

"Call me Chuck. I'm not that much older than you."

"Okay . . . I will, but would you start calling me Christine? That's my real name . . . not Chris."

"Well, Christine, I grabbed a few things to hopefully make your stay here a little better."

"I see that, but I don't really understand. You've already done so much for me. Can we go inside and talk a minute before you leave again?"

"Sure . . . but let me carry these boxes inside first."

"I'll help you," she offered but couldn't help wondering what was inside them.

Once the boxes were taken inside, Christine asked, "Would you like a hamburger sandwich? I'd just started eating when hearing the sound of tires out front."

"No thanks, Darlin'. I had an early dinner. Why don't you finish eating, while I unpack the boxes?"

After uttering a reluctant, "Okay," Christine watched Chuck begin to open several boxes and remove numerous items. Even though the articles weren't wrapped, she felt as though it was like a Christmas morning she'd never experienced . . . full of excitement and curiosity.

As she continued to watch in wonderment, Chuck placed a radio and then a phonograph player on the table. Since placed so close to where she was sitting, she caught herself with her mouth wide open . . . partially chewed food exposed. Stunned beyond words, she watched in amazement each time Chuck opened another box. The biggest box contained pillows, pink sheets, pink pillow cases, and a beautiful floral comforter.

With a big smile, he asked, "Do you like what you see so far?"

Almost choking, she tried to swallow before uttering, "This is so amazing."

"Good, cuz I wanted to amaze you," he answered with a big smile.

A smaller box containing towels, hand towels, and wash clothes was placed beside her chair. She picked up a towel and rested it against her face. It was the softest and fluffiest towel she'd ever felt. Not knowing what to say, she uttered a hushed, "Oh my."

Another box was soon opened . . . revealing toilet paper, paper towels, hand soap, dish soap, miscellaneous cooking utensils, scissors, a can opener, and a couple of packs of cards. Bending forward, she was able to see several records in their jackets but had no clue who the artists were or what kind of music it was. Glancing again at the toilet paper, she was both flabbergasted and appreciative to realize that he'd noticed the lack of toilet paper. How sensitive was that? Finally, the last box was opened, revealing an assortment of can goods. She instantly recognized many familiar soup names. Lastly, he pulled out a small heater.

Hoping Chuck didn't notice her questioned look, the heater didn't make sense. After all, it was barely September . . . so why the heater?

When she looked up, Chuck asked, "Well, what do you think?"

"It's amazing, but I don't understand. So much wonderful stuff, but I don't plan to be here very long."

"I know you'll be leaving soon, but I wanted you to be comfortable while you were staying here . . . even for only a short time."

"Do you mind if I ask you a few questions?" she calmly inquired.

"Of course not . . . shoot," Chuck answered quickly . . . almost like he was expecting questions.

Even without her list of questions, she thought . . . here goes.

"It's not cold now, and I want to be gone before it gets cold. So . . . why the heater?" she asked bluntly.

"Well, I remember the flyer saying you were seventeen but couldn't remember when you'd turn eighteen. I got the heater just in case you wanted to stay until your birthday . . . whenever it was. Also, my boss mentioned moving some young steers in this direction . . . thinking when you left, I might stay here off and on myself."

"Sorry for asking but that makes total sense. My birthday isn't until December. I really want to get to San Antonio before then but don't want to get caught and sent back. So, do you mind if I ask you a few more questions?"

"You can ask me anything. Remember, I'm here to help you."

"Okay then . . . whose pickup truck is that? It's not the one you fetched me in."

"It's my boss's truck. I'm not sure why, but he wanted to personally rustle up some loose bulls that had roamed into a rough area. He didn't want to mess up his truck, so we traded."

Ducking her head and pausing a moment to think of another question, she asked embarrassedly, "How can you afford to help me with all of these gifts? It's too much."

"What else do I have to spend my money on? I look at this as fun and helping out a damsel-in-distress. Oh yeah,

I would have brought you a TV but there's no service this far out." Frowning, Chuck looked directly at her before continuing. "Is something wrong? You look bewildered. If you're afraid or want to go back to Bob's, it's no problem. Again, I just want to help you."

"Where are my manners?" she asked . . . wanting to change the subject. "Would you like something to drink? Not many choices, but I still have a little orange juice left."

"Oh dear . . . I forgot. I brought a couple of sacks of groceries with me. They're in the truck. Hang on! I'll be right back."

When Chuck returned, he was carrying a sack under each arm and clutching a small bottle of vodka in his right hand. Visions of her father drinking made her feel uneasy, but what could she say after all he'd done and given her?

Setting the bags down on the floor beside the table, Chuck asked, "Would you mind if I had a small vodka and orange juice before I leave?"

"Sure, but I don't know how to fix it. Also, there's only a couple of plastic glasses here. Will that be okay for you to use."

"That's fine. I don't need anything fancy. I'll just have one, cuz I'll be driving a long ways."

As she watched him pour vodka into the juice and drink it without stirring, she wondered what he'd do next. While setting the glass down, he asked, "Can I help you put things away?"

"No thanks," she quickly answered before following with, "I'll have lots of time after you leave." Then she quickly added, "Not much else for me to do here abouts."

"Let's play some cards when I come next time? I'd stay longer but need to take my boss's truck back to him. I hope he was successful in herding those crazy bulls back to where they belong. He was sure looking forward to it. You know what I'm thinking . . . he didn't have near as much fun as I've had being with you."

Baffled by what he'd said, she replied, "Really, cuz I'm thinking I had the most fun of all . . . like ever. It was like Christmastime." She almost said she'd never had a decent Christmas, because her Christmases were always messed up. Instead, she said, "Thank you so much."

"A thank you is not necessary. I better be on my way," Chuck responded in a kind manner.

Walking behind Chuck to the door seemed awkward. She'd wanted to ask him about his life, where he lived, did he have a family, and the important question . . . was he married? Instead, she stammered, "When might I see you again?"

His answer seemed guarded when he said, "Probably two weeks . . . maybe three. Don't fret none, cuz I'll come back to make sure you're okay." As an afterthought, he threw her a kiss.

Shutting the door, all she could think about was how Chuck was the greatest and nicest person she'd ever met. Darn it, she'd forgotten to ask so many things but how did she forget to talk to him about letting Bob know she was okay. Next time she saw Chuck; she'd do a better job of planning ahead. In fact, as soon as everything was put away, she'd keep her list in plain sight on the kitchen table. Wow, his visit had been above and beyond exciting. Not only that, but she already found herself missing him, and it was more than just being alone again.

Chapter 12

Kendra quit reading and pushed back from the table. Chastising herself for her automatic sordid evaluation of her mother's new friend, he seemed to be sincerely trying to help. Besides, she shouldn't compare everyone to Albert, she thought and sighed. While thinking about the many differences between Chuck and Albert, Tim and Tim's helpfulness suddenly came to mind. Deciding she was in the right frame of mind to give Tim a call—he said it would be okay—she walked into the kitchen to grab her phone. Why not call him . . . she wanted to; so do it.

Feeling thirsty and before sitting down to call, Kendra opened the refrigerator. When seeing the bottle of orange juice, she couldn't keep from smiling . . . wondering what orange juice and vodka tasted like together. Having never tasted vodka before, she'd buy some vodka and do some experimenting. Why not buy some . . . she wanted to; so she would.

While listening to the rings and waiting for Tim to pick up, Kendra began to waver on her impromptu decision to call. After all, she hadn't given a single thought to what she'd say when he answered, so maybe it wasn't such a good idea and should hang up.

When Tim said, "Hello," she momentarily froze before stammering, "Hi, this is Kendra . . . ah, Kendra Smith."

"Hi Kendra . . . I recognized your number."

"Am I interrupting anything?"

"No, actually my daddy and I were just talking about you. Were your ears burning?"

Wondering what exactly they'd been discussing about her, she hesitantly asked, "Is everything okay?"

"Of course it is. I was just telling my daddy how you were diligently reading your mother's notes found in the trunk. So . . . how's that going? Are you about finished with them?"

While Kendra thought of the best way to explain why it was going so slowly, Tim asked, "Oh, before you tell me, would you mind if I put you on speaker, so my daddy can listen in?"

"That's fine, cuz I'm sure he knows a lot more about what transpired in my mother's past than I do. As far as my digging into Mother's notes; it's kinda hard to tell. It's taking a lot longer than I'd originally imagined . . . one step forward, then one step back. However, I have learned a lot—I think—about how and why she ended up at that house. For instance I've learned why she ran away from home and that she was befriended by a ranch hand who had access to the house. According to her notes, her plan was to stay for only a short time and then go on to college in San Antonio."

"Interesting," was Tim's short reply.

"I'm sorry for talking so much, but Tim . . . it's your fault. You were really easy to talk to when I was in Texas, and I've missed our conversations."

"Really, cuz I was under the impression you couldn't wait to get home and be alone. Remember . . . you'd contact me when you were ready to talk."

Saying, "Okay," but thinking Tim was right; she continued, "Back to Mother's notes . . . which are very difficult and time consuming to put together . . . constantly piecing the scribbled sentences together, so they somewhat make sense. I've been reading them like it's the story of her time there, but sometimes it's hard to believe. One thing for sure, the process helps me grasp what her life was like then. It's been so many years since she was there, and she's saying the house seemed deserted even then. I can't help but wonder if it's even been lived in since she stayed there. Maybe your father knows more about that."

When there was no answer from either Tim or his father, Kendra continued, "I'm sure it's hard for others to understand, but my mother never offered to tell me anything about her life back then . . . treating it like everything was none of my business. I finally just quit asking. That's why I'm doing my best to read every single word in order to decipher what really happened. At this point, I have a feeling that Mother will continue to stay at that house a lot longer than she'd originally planned. Oh dear, I'm sorry for going on and on again."

"I wish we could help you but my father only came into the picture later."

"About that . . . maybe your father can help me."

"How so?" Tim asked.

"Well, when exactly did your father meet my mother? Like . . . how old was my mother when your father met her? Was she living at that house? Let's see . . . was I born then. Who did he draw up the trust with? I mean . . . whose name or names are in the trust . . . especially who is the Grantor or Settlor?"

"Wow, so many questions. Sounds like you've looked up how trusts work?"

"Yes and no . . . but sorta. I wanted to familiarize myself with the basics, so I'd know what questions to ask after finishing Mother's notes. I did make a list of several questions, but I don't have them in front of me right now. "

"I'm looking at my father. He's staying quiet but is shrugging his shoulders. Hang on a moment, so I can ask exactly what the shrugging means."

Kendra listened to a muffled short conversation . . . wondering if Tim had purposely kept his father's answer from her.

"Father said he'd be happy to tell you anything you want to know. That is . . . from what he knows from the time he got involved in the trust process. He and I are both still in the opinion that your mother's wishes were for you read the contents in the trunk first. Having offered our opinions, we both feel that it is definitely your call. Nothing is binding regarding the trust now that your mother has passed. I hope that makes sense, but before you answer, we both want to make finalizing the trust as easy as possible on you. To that end, we will certainly abide by your wishes right now or in the future."

"I guess I should wait. It did seem important to Mother. Maybe it will be easier for me to understand why she was always so hard on me. In her letters, she kept asking for my forgiveness," popped out unexpectedly. "Oh dear, please disregard my last remark. Guess I was just thinking out loud and shouldn't have said that."

"No problem," Tim replied quickly. "You can say or tell us anything."

"Okay, I should let you gentlemen go. Oh yeah . . . I do have one last request. Does the name "Chuck" mean anything to either one of you? That's the name of the ranch hand—according to what she wrote—that's giving refuse to my mother."

When there was no answer, Kendra asked, "Just in case there's somehow a connection, would one of you tell me the name of the Grantor of the trust. If I'm correct, that's the person who sets up the trust in the first place. I'm assuming my mother was the beneficiary."

After a momentary pause, Tim's father chimed in for the first time. "Hi Kendra, this is John Blevins. The name of the Grantor is: Charles Wesley Clayborne . . . the third."

After asking him to spell the name and being careful to write the name down correctly, Kendra said, "Thank you, Mr. Blevins, and I'm glad to talk to you again. I'm sorry we weren't able to meet when I was in Texas."

"Nice talking to you Kendra . . . you take care now."

"Tim uttered quickly, "Kendra, don't hang up. I want to know how it's going besides the tedious reading. How are you doing and is your vacation just about over?"

"I'm doing okay. Thanks for asking. I just want to get this behind me, so I can move on."

"Remember, I'm more than happy to help."

"I appreciate that . . . I truly do."

"So, let's talk more often . . . okay?"

"I'm due to go back to work pretty soon, so I'm hoping to have everything settled before then. Oh, another question . . . ah, sorry. After finishing up with Mother's notes, how long do you think it will take to finish up with the trust and do whatever else is necessary?"

"At this point, the trust is pretty straight forward. The stipulations were all on your mother. Basically, your main concern will be the disposition of the assets . . . ah, mostly the house. There is also a small savings account tied to the trust. How about this . . . you can call me when you finish. No, better yet, call me whenever . . . anytime . . . even if you're not finished. When you're ready, I can come to you, you can come to me, or we can meet in between."

"In between . . . where would that be," she asked seriously.

"I'm kidding about that part. I just wanted you to know it would be your choice,"

"Sorry, I tend to take things literally."

After concluding the call, Kendra was left with mixed emotions. Did she do the right thing by not pressing to get more information? Was it the right thing to wait until finishing her mother's notes? What should she eventually do with the house? Who would want to buy it? It seems totally worthless. Oh well, Tim would surely help guide her at that point.

Being candid with herself, she had missed talking to Tim more than she'd originally considered. Not only that, but she looked forward to seeing him again. No decision needed; she'd travel to Texas to go over the trust. Even better, it was also interesting that she'd been unusually talkative . . . guessing her therapist would consider her talking more and being more outgoing as proof of progress. Although not getting as many answers as she would have liked, the interaction with Tim and his father had been fun. Tomorrow would be her last therapy session for a few weeks as her therapist was going on vacation.

Having the choice to see someone else, she had declined. Usually looking forward to their candid sessions, this time would be both different and difficult. They would be discussing her feelings about returning to work. Since that particular subject hadn't been discussed in some time—having completely put returning to work out of her thoughts—she was full of negative feelings.

Even though Tim had always said she could tell him anything, she had purposely let him think she'd been on an extended vacation. Not even close to the truth, she'd not wanted to open herself up to inquiries about her time off.

After leaving the hospital, she'd been given a few options. Option one was to return immediately to work. Her therapist was against it . . . saying she didn't think she was ready. Option two was to go on unemployment insurance but returning to work would not be guaranteed. Concerned about the lesser pay and her ability to pay the bills, she remembered the difficulty in finding a job in the first place. Option three was taking a medical paid leave of absence. It was less money but in the long run seemed like the best option at the time. She was especially relieved when her medical bills and the therapist sessions were paid by the company.

Since the Albert debacle and her mother's death had happened during the same time period, looking back to that time was like reliving a nightmare in reverse.

So, what did she want to do right now . . . at this very moment? Should she go back to examining her mother's notes . . . no? Should she look at the question list to see what she should have asked Tim and his father on the phone . . . no? Should she do research on the Grantor's name to see what she might discover . . . nope? Smiling, all of that could wait for now. She was off to the store to check out the liquor department . . . looking to purchase her first bottle of vodka. Smiling again, progress was buying booze, and that was uppermost on her mind. Really?

When the call was disconnected, Tim looked questionably at his daddy before asking, "So what's the deal with this Chuck guy?"

"It doesn't take a rocket scientist to figure that out, and Kendra will figure it out on her own when following her mother's notes. Chuck is Charles Wesley Clayborne, who was and still is, an extremely wealthy individual.

"Hmm, so I'm assuming the trust was set up for Kendra, and her mother couldn't tell her anything."

"Correct, and at one time her mother asked my advice about keeping her out of relationships, and away from anyone who might ask questions for fear of losing the money, and etcetera. Naturally, I gave her my two cents worth. She didn't like what I had to say and basically told me to mind my own business of paying the bills and butt out of anything personal with her daughter. She was a bitter individual, but I still felt sorry for her and for Kendra."

Tim's response was another, "Hmm," followed by, "That's food for thought."

Chapter 13

As Kendra dressed and prepared for her therapy session, she stopped to remove a file from the bottom dresser drawer. Months ago, when returning from the hospital, she'd convinced herself that keeping the file stashed away—not seeing it or reading it—would help diminish the panic attacks and hasten her recovery time. She'd only looked at it one time before—and then only briefly—determined to ignore the demoralizing episode contained in the file. Although paying no attention to the file had lessoned her anxiety, it hadn't made the event any easier to forget.

Flipping through the paperwork, Kendra finally arrived at the section about the pros and cons of returning to work. Faced with the reasons for taking so much time off—or much needed time off . . . so she'd been told—

she came across the clipped together papers regarding her mother's car accident. Even though she'd been living on her own and responsible for all aspects of her life, her mother's death affected her more than she'd thought possible. And even though they seldom talked, she wasn't prepared to be completely alone without a single relative anywhere in her life. Since her mother was fairly young—in her early fifties and in good health—her passing had been an incredible shock. And although her mother's death was unexpected, Kendra was grateful the accident took her life immediately, and that she'd not suffered.

Realizing it was still over an hour before her appointment; Kendra began thinking about physically walking into work, and what that would be like. Thoughts began to rush through her head like wondering if any workers would actually remember her. Would they notice her physical appearance had changed? But the big question—getting down to the nitty-gritty—how many workers had viewed the awful pictures distributed throughout social media?

Noticing a page was loose and obviously out of place, Kendra started to flip it over unread. Too late and taking a closer look, it was filled with remarks from the first psychologist's evaluation at the hospital. She must have received the report before leaving the hospital or maybe not. She just couldn't remember. That was such an awful time back then . . . wishing she could just put that terrible ordeal back into the dresser drawer and magically forget it ever happened. But unlike her situation then and where she found herself now, Kendra felt oddly pushed to read the therapist's comments . . . even curious and mentally prepared. Starting from the top and reading downward: lack of self-confidence, introverted, no social skills, stunted maturity, and . . . on and on. Scanning quickly to the last entry: post traumatic stress disorder . . . past and present. Hmm, past and present . . . what did that mean?

Hopefully, this coming session with her present therapist would help her return to work without having a major meltdown. What would she have done without the therapist's guidance? She had been such a blessing to her healing process. Above all, she'd given her hope for a normal and happy future.

Without meaning to go back in time, Kendra found herself remembering.

* * * *

Having run out of viable excuses, Kendra finally agreed on a date and time to meet Albert. She didn't want him to pick her up, preferring to meet at his suggested spot . . . a bar and local hang-out for young working adults called "Fun Times." As she'd never been there before—more specifically, any bar before—she had relied on Albert's choice and preference. Albert had assured her that it was a great place to go; a place where they could comfortably talk and further their relationship. He kept telling her, "It's going to be a lot of fun to talk to you in person."

Bottom line, she was not only apprehensive about meeting him at a bar but also afraid of meeting him—or any man anywhere—due to her lifetime of various insecurities.

Having already looked up the place on the internet, the inside pictures were difficult to see because of the lack of lighting. She'd hoped her plan of meeting inside a dimly lit establishment would be better. Knowing she was early—as she always tried to be and always was—Kendra could feel herself shaking. When she opened the door, she felt so awkward that she was unable to step inside. Instead of entering, she immediately turned around and left.

Walking back to her car, Kendra began talking to herself about being a coward. Of course she'd expected to be nervous but really wanted to meet Albert . . . no matter how it turned out. So, if she didn't go through with their plan to meet, Albert might never speak to her again. There was absolutely no way she could let that happen. After all, Albert was the only friend she'd ever had. For this single instance in her life, this was her now or never moment.

Kendra waited in her car for an exasperating twenty minutes . . . talking constantly to herself. As she watched the clock, she noticed it was beginning to get dark outside;

telling herself that if she left right now, she would arrive exactly at the planned meeting time.

When Kendra opened the door for the second time—she actually looked inside; finding it darker inside than outside. Having not described herself, she should have wondered why Albert immediately waved to her before motioning her over to his table. As she approached, she concentrated on carefully maneuvering her way through several nearby tables. Glancing in Albert's direction, he was not what she expected. He appeared much younger than she'd expected, but knew he wouldn't find her what he'd imagined either. Feeling unattractive and out of place, Kendra tried to smile but considered turning around and running back out the door, getting into her car, and never seeing or talking to Albert again.

Albert continued to stand awkwardly while she pulled out her own chair and sat down. Perhaps Albert noticed how uncomfortable she was feeling, because he reached over and covered her shaking hands with his. His warm touch was calming but also gave her a strange and previously unknown tingling feeling. Unable to find the right words to say, she mumbled a quiet, "Thank you," while thinking . . . that sounded stupid. What in the world had she thanked him for . . . meeting her, reaching out to take her shaking hands, or both?

Kendra couldn't exactly remember what they talked about, but it wasn't long before he offered the memorized put-down remark, "You're not as ugly as I thought you were."

She did, however, easily recall becoming thirsty and asking for a coke to drink. However, Albert ignored her request and returned with something different . . . definitely not a coke.

Noticing the glass looked strange for a coke; she took a sip and grimaced.

Frowning, he asked, "Is something wrong?"

"Sorta . . . I guess. I don't know what this is, but it's not coke."

"Oh, I'm sorry. I got us both the same drink." Pointing to his own drink, Albert offered, "See, I'm having the same thing."

So far out of her comfort zone, Kendra didn't know exactly how to respond but was determined to be sociable. Having no clue about alcohol drink names, she asked, "What is this drink called?"

"I don't know if it has an official name, but it's a combination of whiskey and coke. I'm a beer drinker myself but thought a different drink would be a good start to our meeting. I'm thinking it will help us both relax and get to know each other better. Alcohol is said to hinder you inhibitions, so that way we can tell each other our deepest secrets. Isn't that what friends are for?" Albert said with a big smile.

"Well, I'm not used to drinking alcohol." Pausing to take another sip, she continued. "It tastes awful."

"I'd say it's best to take it down like medicine. That's what I've been told," Albert offered.

"I'll try. Maybe it will taste better once I get used to it."

"I can take it back if you want me to. I just want you . . . us to have a good time together."

No way did Kendra want to disappoint Albert, so quickly replied, "You're right, so here goes." After swallowing a big gulp, Kendra thought she'd surely throw up. "Do you know where the girl's room is?" Kendra asked, feeling her eyes watering.

"Sure, it's to the right side of the bar," Albert answered before pointing to the bar area.

Hurrying away and praying she wouldn't vomit before reaching the bathroom; she rushed in to slap cold water on her face and then rinsed out her mouth. As she gargled, she wondered how she could sneak out without Albert noticing. As she thought about leaving, she already knew how improper that would be. After all, it wasn't Albert's fault that she was such a looser. What a mess she'd made of this in-person meeting. It was a total disaster, her fault, and she hated herself and her life.

As Kendra returned to the table, determined to tell Albert she was leaving, she noticed a different drink in a different shaped glass in front of where she'd been sitting. After sitting down—again pulling out her own chair—Albert said, "I'm sorry. I got you a plain coke this time."

"Thank you so much. I guess I would be considered a light weight."

Not commenting on her remark, Albert reached out and patted her arm before asking in a kind manner, "What would make you happy to talk about?" Before replying, Kendra thought maybe her very first date in her entire life would turn out being a pleasant one after all.

Beginning to have a good time and feeling more comfortable, they talked about similar topics already discussed over the phone. Although much younger than she was, Albert was similar in many ways. He didn't discuss his home life, his relatives . . . actually nothing about anything personal and—like her—almost secretive. Finishing her coke—actually downing it—she asked, "Do you think it's getting warm in here?"

"No, but it might be the company you're keeping that's heating you up," he answered with a quizzical look and a wink.

"Perhaps the alcohol in the first drink is affecting me. Do you think that's possible?"

"No, I don't think so . . . you only had a little bit. Would you like another coke?"

"Yes, I'm really thirsty," was Kendra's quick answer.

Drinking about half of the coke, she uttered, "I'm beginning to feel very tired . . . ah, sleepy. I'm so very sorry. This isn't like me, and you must think I'm a total bore. I think I better go home."

"Okay, let me walk you to your car. Maybe some fresh air will help you feel better."

Everything around her began to move in slow motion. With the room swaying, she appreciated Albert placing his arm around her waist and helping her walk outside.

Slurring her words, Kendra mumbled, "I don't think I can walk any further . . . can't hardly stay awake. I don't understand. I've never been like this before."

As her staggering got worse, Albert said, "Here's my van. It's closer than your car. Let me help you get inside, so you can rest a minute. When you feel better, I'll help you to your car. You'll be fine. Trust me . . . I'll take care of you."

She garbled something impossible to understand before completely passing out.

* * *

Waking in the hospital, Kendra knew nothing past leaving the bar. Disoriented, she had several bazaar flashbacks about odd images, but they were like combinations of bad dreams.

Kendra was told that she'd been found by the side of the road by a couple returning from a late night dinner at 11:37 PM. They had called for an ambulance and stated to the arriving paramedics, "It was terrible. We found her laying there naked with her clothes piled up beside her."

When Kendra tried to explain what happened, it was impossible to distinguish between what was real and what wasn't. She felt too embarrassed to talk about her weird recollections of her face being licked, the floating about of a Champaign bottle, or the surrounding flashing stars that burst around her. It was impossible to share those images with the attending physician without the fear of him thinking she was nuts. Her additional scary thought . . . maybe she was. Finally, she offered, "I can't remember what happened. I just can't remember anything."

Shortly after, a female doctor appeared at the door and asked if they could talk? She seemed genuinely kind when Kendra told her she couldn't remember anything passed leaving the bar.

"That makes perfect sense, because you were roofied and sexually assaulted."

Not familiar with the term "roofied," Kendra pathetically said, "Oh no! Can I be pregnant?" She then quickly added, "I don't take birth control pills."

"No, we did a rape test and other appropriate tests to determine what happened to you. It appears that you were given a "date rape" drug, and you show minor damages due to a foreign object or objects. The police have already been notified, and they will come in to interview you before you're released to go home. Also, our resident psychologist will be in to talk to you later. In the meantime, we will continue to monitor you by flushing out your system of the drug and giving you pain medication by mouth and antibiotics for your injuries . . . mostly swollen tissue and a few minor abrasions to your vagina . . . nothing permanent or life threatening."

Frowning, Kendra asked, "Wouldn't I know if I was given a drug?"

"Not necessarily because it's both tasteless and odorless," was answered quickly.

Kendra remembered—like it happened yesterday—of being utterly bewildered; realizing how Albert had taken advantage of her while pretending to be her friend and planning to hurt her. Her mother's words returned over and over again, "Never trust a man."

Not remembering exactly what time the police came in to interview her, she did remember how foolish she felt. She again told them how she didn't remember anything after leaving the bar. She tried to tell them as much as she knew about him, while feeling embarrassed about how little she actually knew. She didn't know his last name and wasn't sure if he'd given her the correct first name. She met him on the internet, and he said he was a data processer. Whether that was true or not; he did seem to know a lot about data gathering. She told them his telephone number but admitted to never calling him. She gave them the name of the bar . . . hoping they had security cameras present. Even better and if he was a regular customer there, maybe they could identify him. Before the interview concluded, the detective said, "We will do our best to find him, but honestly you shouldn't get your hopes up. In my opinion, he sounds like he's done this before." The other detective bluntly added, "Don't be so trusting next time."

Depressed and knowing the upcoming therapy session was bound to bring up additional unpleasant memories, Kendra returned the file to the dresser drawer.

While driving to her appointment, Kendra tried to think of how she felt secure with Tim, but Albert's actions kept over-shadowing Tim's kindnesses. When Kendra walked into the office—five minutes late—the psychologist immediately asked, "Okay, what's the matter?"

Chapter 14

Kendra sat down on the closest chair and began to cry.

Perplexed, the therapist offered, "It's okay to be a tad late. Hopefully nothing is wrong. If you're okay and remembering your obsession with tardiness, I find your lateness refreshing."

Ignoring her remark, Kendra blurted out, "I thought I was doing all right until glancing through the file about my time at the hospital and . . . well, you know . . . Albert."

"Remember, he doesn't deserve a name. He's a perpetrator. Let's refer to him as Slime Bag, Cow Dung, or better yet . . . Ass Hole. Smiling, she said, "Sorry, I'm going on vacation tomorrow and practicing on leaving my therapy hat behind." Pausing to see what Kendra's reaction was, she followed with, "I'm proud of you for looking at the file. You said you were going to hide it away and hadn't looked at it except for briefly one time. I see this as good news for facing it again."

"Really?" was Kendra's thoughtful reply."

"So . . . did returning to work bring the past up?"

"I guess; I was so stupid then. I never questioned anything."

"Kendra, that's all in the past. Remember we talked about the only way to change a mistake is to want to and then not repeat it. I think we need to talk about handling the present. It's all about moving forward and being positive about your life now and planning for the future."

"I'm trying to but how can I go back to work and act like nothing happened."

"Because you can; that's how. Your actions are under your control . . . remember that. Have you finished with your mother's notes yet?"

"No, not yet," Kendra answered in a somewhat ashamed manner.

"So, I'm assuming the trust hasn't been settled either."

Looking across the desk, Kendra's reply was a disgusted shake of her head accompanied by a frown.

"This sounds to me like you're dealing with a lot on your plate right now. If I'm looking at your timeline, you planned to have all of this settled before returning to work. Is that correct?"

"You're right. I'm not trying to put it off on purpose . . . if that's what you mean. It's just taking longer than I originally thought."

"Obviously, something is bothering you, and it has nothing to do with arriving here late. I'm thinking it must have to do with returning to work, so let's address that before my time away. When is your first day back to work?"

"Next Monday," Kendra answered quickly.

"So, let's talk about that and the steps to making it easier and so forth. I'm sure you've already thought about it in depth and realize how different it will be. You'll be wearing different types of clothing, your hair is styled differently, you'll be wearing makeup, and no glasses.

Above all, you are different both inside and out for all the reasons we've discussed in our sessions. You are a competent and attractive young woman who has been able to hold onto the thoughtful person who has always been within you . . . but now much more cautious."

Kendra continued to look down at the floor and took awhile to answer. "I don't think I'm ready. I might look different but don't feel different sometimes."

"Have you checked in with Human Resources yet or do you plan to go straight into your previous work area?"

"I don't know, cuz I haven't even considered calling. I'd just assumed I'd go back like before, but you know what . . . that's a good idea. I should call first."

"That would be my suggestion. That way, you'll know exactly how to proceed."

"I'll call as soon as I get home," Kendra answered with a nod.

"My other suggestion would be to walk in with confidence . . . like you're any other employee and belong there. Look preoccupied with a file or piece of paper if you begin to feel uncomfortable and—more or less—ignore others. I'd imagine they'll be dealing with their own Monday morning rush schedules anyway."

"What if they saw the pictures?"

"So what! Yes, they were explicit but not dwelled on like you've done. It was personal for you and devastating, but whoever saw them has long ago moved on to something else."

"But you've seen them. They were so awful"

"Let me ask you another question. Are you upset that A Hole hasn't been caught and arrested?"

"Yes, of course I am."

"I agree but during court proceedings, the pictures would have been distributed and viewed by more people. You would have endured additional scrutiny and embarrassment. It's in the past."

Kendra finally replied, "What if he does that to another unsuspecting person?"

"Let's hope that more people are becoming aware of how to protect themselves from that sort of thing. Maybe you can eventually get involved in anonymously helping to get the word out about date rape drugs and the best way for others to protect themselves." Pausing and looking directly at Kendra, she asked, "Are you feeling any better?"

"I think so. I will call Human Resources. Thanks for that suggestion."

"I'm going to give you my private telephone number just in case you have a problem and need immediate attention."

"I won't bother you. I hope you enjoy your time away from nutty people like me."

"Don't be silly. I am extremely proud of how you've improved, and I look forward to your continual progress. I'm equally as happy to have been here to help you along your journey of becoming the person you were always meant to be. Is there anything else you want to discuss?"

"No, that's about it."

"Kendra, I wish you good luck. Keep smiling no matter what . . . okay?"

"I'll try and thanks."

Kendra sat in the car, feeling somewhat uplifted. Leaving her usual therapy sessions always made her feel better but today was especially rewarding. She'd gone from feeling insecure about returning to work to ready to tackle it—head on—no matter what the outcome.

She decided to stop and do a little shopping . . . thinking she wanted to purchase a new outfit for Monday. After that, she'd stop and pick-up something fattening at a nearby drive-thru. A cheeseburger and fries with a chocolate milkshake sounded perfect.

Leaving the parking lot, she thought with a big smile . . . watch out world, Kendra is on the move.

Chapter 15

Having laid out her new outfit early, Kendra found herself ready for work in plenty of time. Her Monday morning was going along too quickly, so she needed to slow down. If she didn't, she'd be early or maybe exactly on time. It was really difficult to change habits created over the years, but she'd keep trying. Having been told that being on time is considered admirable but fixating on it to the point that it ruins everything else is considered excessive/compulsive behavior.

Purposely arriving two minutes late for her appointment at nine o'clock, Kendra began to give herself a pep talk. Glancing around and doing her best to remain calm and act confident, she reached for the door handle. "Okay here goes," she said out loud in a determined fashion. As she opened the door and entered the building, she looked to see if anyone appeared to be watching her. As all seemed fine, so far . . . so good, she thought. While walking through the lobby area, so far . . . so good, she thought again. True to the therapist's words . . . the other employees seemed preoccupied with getting to their work stations, so no one seemed to be paying any attention to her.

During the pleasant phone call with the lady in Human Resources, she was asked to first stop by and talk to them before reporting to work. At that time, they would discuss a new project they were considering. While knowing Human Recourses was located on the third floor, she couldn't remember exactly where it was located. Instead of freaking out for not asking for the unit number during the phone conversation, she would take a new and rare approach . . . if she couldn't find it, she'd stop and ask someone for help. Aware that others would think this was the normal thing to do; this way of handling something new would be another milestone in her life. How her attitudes had changed from before . . . progress in action, she thought with a smile.

Not feeling relaxed but not feeling insecure either . . . like in the past, she walked up to the counter and smiled before saying, "Hi, I'm Kendra Smith and have a nine o'clock appointment. Sorry, I'm a tad late."

"Welcome back to the grind," was answered with a smile.

"I was told to report here to Mrs. Snider before returning to my regular spot."

"Yes, our supervisor . . . Mrs. Snider . . . wants to talk with you about a couple of options . . . like was briefly discussed on the phone call. Come on back to her office. Follow me . . . okay."

After the usual introductions were exchanged, the supervisor said, "First of all, my condolences and the company's for your mother's passing."

While answering, "Thank you, I appreciate that;" Kendra was concentrating on the particulars of their earlier phone call. Also, going first to Human Resources had taken away some of her initial anxiousness about returning to her previous work station. Although stopping there was delaying the inevitable, she also knew it was impossible to completely ignore. Being back in the building was bringing up so many emotions. No matter how hard she tried, the thought of the people working directly with her had—most likely—seen the pictures on social media or at least heard about them.

Continuing, Mrs. Snider said, "Secondly, the company is sincerely sorry for your necessary medical leave." Not elaborating which left Kendra wondering what she meant, Mrs. Snider immediately said, "Okay, let's move on. While you were off, we did a review of your work and the associated data. Your production numbers were especially impressive . . . much better than any of the other departments. We are in the process of setting up a new department on data information connected to fuel costs, shipping, and the related transportation costs. It's important information to be gathered because all facets of industry are eventually affected. Because of your impressive work, we would like to offer you the new position of Assistant to the company's Production Manager. Basically, you would be the head person for the new department. You will also receive a substantial pay raise. At first, your staff will be small but hopefully will increase depending on the number of requests generated for out-put. If you're interested, I'll go over the particulars with you. If not, we have kept your old position open for you."

"I'm stunned, and hardly know what to say," was Kendra's immediate response. I'm definitely interested but want to know a little more before I answer for sure."

After more details were discussed and finding no negatives, Kendra agreed to the new arrangement before finally saying, "I'll do my best to be productive and appreciate the trust you've placed in me."

On the drive back home, Kendra felt confident that she'd made an easy final decision on the new position. Even after the original phone discussion with Human Resources—and before knowing the full details associated with the job—she had already decided to take the new assignment. She considered the pay increase discussed at today's meeting an extra bonus. Above everything else, she was extremely proud of herself for ultimately making the decision with only a brief hesitation. If able to talk with her psychologist, she'd have told her about making an almost a spur-of-the-moment decision during the phone call and then following through at the meeting without fixating on it for days.

Chapter 16

Returning home and feeling giddy, Kendra wondered if her emotion was what real happiness felt like, and wished she had someone to share the good news with. Reconsidering, she could call Tim, but he was sure to ask if she'd finished her mother's notes yet, and was she ready to move on to reviewing the trust. Well, today was about celebrating her new position by doing something out of the ordinary . . . something new and different; but what? How about ordering a pizza—one with the works on top—and watching a movie during daytime hours? Grinning, she thought . . . this isn't a plan but more like an impromptu party for one . . . and that was fine No, better than fine; it would be lots of fun.

Since Kendra didn't need to begin her newly acquired position until Friday—and then, only for orientation—she'd step away and take a long break from her mother's notes until tomorrow, giving herself extra time for fun.

* * *

Feeling relaxed after pigging out on pizza and watching two movies the following day, Kendra began early Tuesday morning to tackle the notes. When picking up the next note—located not too far from the end of the stack—she tried to remember where she'd left off. Oh yeah, that's right. Her mother was out in that old house by herself, and Chuck had dropped off a bunch of gifts. Again, she thought how Chuck seemed like a nice and decent person. However, as she considered his character, additional questions took her back to wondering what happened. Could Chuck possibly be her father? If so, what if something awful happened to him . . . or worse yet, what if he'd died? Could that possibility be the reason why her mother left Texas or for her mother's sullen attitude throughout her life? What if her mother was so broken-hearted that she'd been unable to talk about him or their early life together? Well, no need to speculate further because Mother obviously wanted her to find out what took place through her notes.

The first few notes were all about how Mother was constantly waiting for Chuck while keeping busy sprucing up the house. She scribbled down how she was decorating it little-by-little and constantly worrying about whether or not Chuck would like it. When she wrote about something she'd done and waiting to see if Chuck approved; she referred to the house as "her house." Reading between the lines—so to speak—Chuck seemed to be there quite often. Her mother mentioned playing cards, listening to music, and even dancing. She seemed happy and no longer mentioned anything about leaving for San Antonio or going to college.

The notes soon began to move along at a faster pace, and the dates were farther and farther apart. Sometimes, weeks would go by without a single entry. Obviously, jotting down her thoughts and observations wasn't a priority like before.

Every time Kendra tried to rush through the notes, she'd miss something that didn't seem significant at the time—but when referenced later—it would be necessary to go back and reread the previous words more carefully.

She remembered reading some time ago about Mother asking Chuck for a tree—wanting to look at something green outside—but hadn't given it much attention until reading today about Mother's excitement when Chuck arrived with a huge Cyprus tree on a flatbed truck with additional men to help plant it . . . placing it beside the house. As she read how glad her mother was about the tree being enormous and writing that it would soon shade the front porch; it was obviously clear that her mother—at that time—wasn't planning on leaving any time soon. Thinking more about it, the tree referenced in the notes had to be the same old tree with the broken branch near the house. Although difficult to gage the tree's age, Kendra knew her mother would have been eighteen years old by then. Also, it had to be the tree where she and Tim located the diamond ring that looked like an engagement ring.

Reading her mother's notes was like reading a book and thinking . . . the plot thickens.

Wow, Kendra hadn't thought about the ring since returning from Texas. It seemed like a good idea to have it appraised before starting back to work. Again, the ring brought up a myriad of thoughts and questions. What if it was worth something and if so, what would she do with it? Why did Mother bury it if it turned out to be valuable? Hopefully, more reading would help her discover answers to the many mysteries about her mother and about her own early existence.

Looking on the internet and wanting to be as meticulous as possible, Kendra checked out various jewelry appraisers in the area. She also wanted to find a reputable company, see their reviews, and make sure they were licensed. After gathering as much information as possible—along with addresses and telephone numbers— she was off to find answers. Walking out the door, she thought how she could be on a treasure hunt or be spending a total waste of time.

Returning home after a long afternoon, Kendra was more confused than ever. The ring was extremely valuable . . . the diamonds worth at least $5,500, and the white gold solitaire setting worth another $500. She had no idea and didn't ask what the ring would have cost when it was given to her mother years ago. She also didn't ask if the appraiser knew the age of the ring. In fact, she didn't even know—for sure—if it was actually given to her mother. If everything was on the up-and-up, why did Mother bury the ring and leave Texas without it? If Chuck gave it to her, how could he afford an expensive ring like that? Worst case scenario, what if the ring was stolen? Kendra considered calling John Blevins to see if he could shine some light on the ring but ultimately decided against it. She would place the ring away again . . . determined not to look at it until after finishing her mother's notes, reading and hopefully understanding the trust, and finalizing the paperwork.

Okay, back to reading more of the notes. The notes suddenly jumped ahead by at least six months, but what stood out more than anything else . . . Mother's words and attitudes seemed different. She sounded more adult and confident. She talked about how Chuck was staying over some nights—usually on the weekends—and how she loved him so much. Without saying exactly what had transpired, she mentioned how Chuck had taught her what being a full-fledged woman was all about, and how caring and gentle he'd been. She wrote how they were spending as much time as possible together and wishing he worked closer. She wrote about being embarrassed when he'd dropped her off at a doctor's office to get birth control pills. She continued to mention—over and over—how much she missed him while he was away, and how much she loved cooking his favorite dishes when he returned . . . especially apple cobbler.

Her mother never wrote anything about the details of how she got groceries, if she had her own transportation, or if she had contact with anyone except Chuck. How did she actually get the birth control pills? Where was the closest drug store? Was she able to send or receive mail?

Again, these questions were among so many that most likely would never be answered.

As Kendra moved the chair back from the table, she glanced at the remaining unread notes still waiting to be deciphered. She would stop for a brief dinner and could possibly finish with them by the end of the day. Her fervent hope would be that once she understood the why, when, and where, she'd be more equipped to deal with the next stage of completing everything and moving on with her own life. She picked up the sheet where she'd added a list of questions to ask . . . placing the word "ring" on it with a question mark. Briefly glancing at the previous entries, she noticed the ring had already been listed . . . so crossed it out. Becoming optimistic, she hoped that by the time she finished with her mother's notes, many more entries could also be crossed off.

After a short break and anxious to return to her mother's notes, a few answers were quickly revealed. At first, Mother gleefully discussed how happy she was . . . even describing how Chuck had asked if she'd marry him and gave wordy and descriptive details on how he'd given her the engagement ring. Along with the ring, he'd given her a single rose and how she'd kept it in a glass of water on the kitchen table . . . even after it died and dried out. She plainly mentioned knowing the ring was most likely glass—assuming he couldn't afford a real diamond—but she didn't care. It was easy to feel her excitement though her written words. Even though Chuck was working long hours and barely had time to visit her, he had become her whole world. She went on and on about how he was looking for a better job, so they could marry and have a proper life together. She continued writing down—over and over—how much she loved him.

Then . . . Kendra opened the last sheet of paper. Actually it was two notebook sized papers folded until they were about the size of a small envelope. It was full of anger and written—per the date—soon after she'd been born. Her mother stated how she'd just returned from San Antonio where she'd given birth to a baby girl and how she was being forced to leave Texas.

Kendra kept rereading the pages in disbelief. Her mother didn't say exactly why or when she had to leave Texas . . . stating many times that it wasn't her choice and repeating how she was being forced to leave. So, apparently Chuck was—or if still alive—would be her father. It sorta made sense but there were additional questions not answered or laid to rest. Kendra began to feel sick because of the many personal unknowns. While going over and over the last sentences, Kendra was not only sick at her stomach but also felt angry and hurt for her mother.

Mother sounded pathetic when writing, "I'm alone and don't know what to do." Kendra couldn't understand what changed after her birth. Since Tim's father and Tim both knew exactly what was contained in the trust—one was involved in the actual writing of the trust and the other admitted to reading it—either one could help her understand exactly what was written in the trust. Although Kendra felt more comfortable with Tim, realistically his father would have a better understanding of the circumstances leading up to the writing of the trust.

Setting her personal feelings aside, it made the most sense to talk with John Blevins first.

As Kendra looked down through her sheet of questions to ask, she came across the name of the Grantor: Charles Wesley Clayborne III. What could she discover about him if she looked for his name on the internet? Could his nickname have been Chuck? Not everyone is listed on the internet but his name sounded sorta important. If nothing else, it was worth a try, Kendra thought. She'd see what she could find out—something or nothing—but would definitely check him out.

Kendra was shocked to find his name so easily on the internet. There were several entries for his name as well as the corporation he represented: Clayborne Cattle Ranch and brand: C C R. He was listed as the CEO and leading partner of the corporation with its head office located in Austin, Texas but supplying beef around the world. It listed him as being the third generation of the founders of the Clayborne Cattle Ranch . . . originally established in Texas. In addition to continuing to raise cattle in Texas for distribution, the corporation now has beef herds scattered throughout Hawaii.

Although the information on the corporation was interesting, Kendra was more curious about what she could locate about him on a personal level. Scrolling carefully down through the listings, she finally came across exactly what she'd been searching for: Bio for Charles Wesley Clayborne III. It listed an abundance of personal information—important for Kendra to learn— like his age, his marital status, the names of his children, etc. It also listed the college he'd graduated from: The University of Texas . . . where the words "Go Longhorns" were added. His age seemed to fit but nothing else looked right. Kendra remembered that her mother knew Chuck was much older but according to the dates listed; he was fourteen years older . . . about thirty-two when her mother was eighteen. Kendra kept rereading the information about the name of his wife, the years they'd been married, and the names and ages of their twin boys. But no matter how she tried to compute the figures, nothing added up. Doubts began to sink in about the man she thought might be her father. While trying to understand why he was listed as the Grantor on the trust, Kendra was feeling totally confused. But if he was her father, then he was already married when asking her mother to marry him. Also, he'd already had two boys when she'd been born. If calculating correctly, they would have been almost three years old at the time of her birth.

Doing her best to wrap her mind around what she'd just read, Kendra saw several small blurbs about how Charles W. Clayborne was exploring the feasibility of becoming a candidate for the District 10 Congressional Seat . . . stretching from the northwestern portion of the Greater Houston region to the Greater Austin region.

Although her stomach had now somewhat settled down; her mind was racing. She hoped she'd be able to eventually sleep tonight and couldn't wait to contact either Tim's father or Tim tomorrow . . . maybe both . . . hopefully both.

Chapter 17

Because she'd been up late researching the man she thought could be her father—and overwhelmed with the information she'd found—Kendra had finally gone to bed in the early hours but slept sporadically . . . waking several times to rehash her discoveries.

By the time she'd showered, had a strawberry breakfast drink, and organized her list of questions to ask; it dawned on her that Texas time was two hours ahead of California time. Looking at the clock again—ten o'clock—their law office could be closed for lunch.

Knowing her curiosity wouldn't let her wait much longer, and just in case the office was still closed on Fridays; she only had today and tomorrow to understand the ending of her mother's stay in Texas. After waiting for years to learn how her own life began, and enduring exasperating days sorting through her mother's notes, waiting a minute longer would seem like forever. If unable to get answers before Friday, she'd be spending a frustrating weekend in limbo until next week.

After waiting for a bothersome hour, Kendra sat down at the dining room table, placed the sheet of questions before her, and made sure her phone was switched to speaker. Taking in a deep breath, she punched in the law office's number.

When the receptionist answered, Kendra quickly asked, "Is either John or Timothy Blevins available?"

"May I ask who's calling?"

"My name is Kendra Smith, and I'm a client of theirs," she replied.

"If you'll hold a moment, I'll check to see if either one is available."

Tim's first words after saying, "Hello stranger" were, "So, you've finished with your mother's notes. Am I right?"

"Yes, but I'm not sure who I should talk to . . . you or your father? I have lots of questions to ask before I delve into reading the trust. Like . . . what happened before the trust was written?"

"I understand . . . thinking you might. Since we last talked, I've had several interesting conversations myself with Daddy."

"Is it possible to have a joint conversation with you both?" Kendra asked.

"Well . . . yes and no. Unfortunately, right at the moment, Daddy has gone fishing again. Having said that, I do believe it's important for you to talk to him. He's been personally involved in helping your mother through some difficult times. Also, Daddy has been directly involved in administering the trust through the years. He has actually been the trustee for the trust."

Disappointed but trying her best not to show it, Kendra responded, "Good for him for going fishing. What's your suggestion on how I can get answers to some of my questions about what happened before the trust was drawn up?"

"First, tell me what your time frame is like? I mean, he's traveling at the moment but when he gets situated; we can have a conference call with him, or I can have him call you. Right now, his phone reception is very poor . . . actually nonexistent. In fact, I've tried to call several times today and couldn't reach him."

"Darn it! I'm returning to work this Friday, and it's already Wednesday afternoon. I'm not sure what to do. I have a lot of questions to ask him but don't want to read the trust yet, and . . . well, you know . . . ."

"I totally understand," Tim replied before adding, "What's your weekend like?"

"What do you mean?" Kendra asked hesitantly.

"Well, Father should be settled in by the weekend. I could fly out and go over the trust."

"I'm sorry, I still don't quite understand," Kendra said . . . totally confused.

"After talking with Father, I can—most likely—answer many of your questions. As for all of the answers, the ones I can't help you with; well, we could then have a conference call with him. I'm just throwing this out as a possibility."

"Well, it doesn't seem right for you to come all this distance just to help me."

"Why not? I like helping you. I could fly out Friday and meet you after you finish work?"

"You'd really do that for me?" Kendra asked in a surprised manner before seriously adding, "I can pay for your trip to meet with me. How would that be?"

"That won't be necessary. I can afford it," Tim replied with a chuckle.

"How would that work out? I mean . . . I'm not sure of my hours on Friday."

"Don't worry about it. I'll figure it out." Tim answered quickly.

"Well, I do worry about it. It's just that it's my first day back, and I'm meeting for orientation to head up a new company division. It will be new to me and new for the company, so I'm not sure if I could meet you at the airport. What is your suggestion?"

"First of all . . . it's not a problem. How about this idea? I have your phone number, and I think your address. Maybe you should give the address to me again . . . just in case. I'll fly in and find a hotel. When you get out of work, you can give me a call. If all works out, we can meet for dinner. Once I book the flight, I'll call you with the information. Does that sound like a plan?" Tim asked.

"Yes, but are you sure?" Kendra questioned.

"I'm very sure. In the meantime, I'll continue to work on making contact with my father. I'll tell you later about what we've already discussed when we meet. I can't wait to see you again. Is there anything else I can help you with . . . before we get off the phone?"

"No, I think that's about it. I've got a lot of questions to ask, but they can wait until I see you. Don't forget to bring the trust. I haven't read Mother's third letter yet. Remember, it's supposed to be the trust. I just want to make sure what she gave me is the same as the original."

Without commenting on Kendra's remark about the trust, Tim replied, "See you soon."

When Kendra disconnected the phone, she was filled with mixed emotions. She was definitely excited about seeing Tim again, but disappointed about not getting answers to the sheet of questions on the table before her. Would Tim's flight get in before or after she got off work? Would he rent a car? Would his hotel be fairly close or across town? It seemed that she was always feeling unsure when it came to Tim, but decided the uncertain feeling was attached to her not doing the actual planning or controlling the situation. Soon—one way or the other—she was determined to get answers to her questions.

It was nearly eight o'clock Thursday morning when Kendra saw an incoming call from Blevins and Blevins Law Firm. When she answered—expecting it to be Tim— Kendra was surprised to hear from an assistant saying, "Good morning! Is this Kendra Smith?"

"Yes, it is," she replied hesitantly.

"I'm calling for Timothy Blevins to give you the following information."

After writing down the name of the airline, the flight number, and the arrival time at LAX, she thanked the caller before saying, "Do you mind if I repeat the information back to you?"

When Kendra finished, the caller said, "You got it. Y'all have a blessed day. Bye, bye now"

Wishing she'd asked why Tim hadn't called her personally, she quickly reminded herself . . . duh, that's really none of my business.

Gosh, she was looking forward to seeing Tim. She had several emotions flowing through her mind. Seeing Tim again, starting a new position at work, learning the reason why her mother left Texas, learning whether or not Charles W. Clayborne III was her father, and actually reading what's in the trust. Today, she needed to make sure the house was presentable—just in case Tim visited—and lay out her clothes for work tomorrow. Thinking about what clothes to wear, she should also decide on outfits to wear while Tim was in town.

* * *

Kendra had no reason to worry about her new work position. She was introduced to her new "crew" who seemed friendly and professional. She liked their enthusiasm, and they seemed to like her willingness to accept feedback. Her immediate boss joined in during their first discussion and raved on her qualifications. Kendra often felt herself smiling but also felt embarrassed to receive so many compliments. After the morning went by quickly, Kendra asked for lunch to be brought in for her new staff. They all seemed sincerely surprised and appreciative of the gesture. By the end of the day, Kendra felt happy to be back at work . . . amazed that it had gone by so easily.

Once settled into the car and before calling Tim, Kendra took a moment to reflect on the day. Why were her emotions so different now? Easy to answer, she was a different person now . . . and that made her smile. So with that in mind and looking forward to seeing Tim again, it was time to call.

When Tim answered, Kendra could almost hear the happiness in his voice. Her life was definitely changing in so many ways and for the better, she thought and smiled again.

"So, where are you," Kendra asked.

"The truth is; I'm out by the pool having a beer," he answered with a chuckle.

"I'm thinking that means you're off the plane and at a hotel . . . right?"

"That's why I like you . . . you're so smart."

"Hmm, so you like me?" Kendra questioned with a giggle.

"Yes ma'am . . . I do."

"So . . . how many beers have you had?" Kendra asked.

"Quite a few actually but who's counting. I'm having a glass after every four laps. However, I must admit that I've recently lost count of both. In my defense, I'm not driving."

"Do you still want to meet this evening for dinner?"

"Of course I do. Didn't I just say . . . ah, I like you? So, doesn't it follow that I want to see you, and I'm always ready to eat."

"You're silly. It must be the beer talking."

"I'll prove it if you'll come see me. I'll even pay for your dinner. That's probably best since I've already confessed to drinking and shouldn't be driving. Could you hurry over cuz I'm really hungry."

"I'm not sure how soon I can be there, since I have no clue where you are," Kendra replied.

"According to my calculations—with a little help from a mapping site—the hotel is a little over three miles from your home address."

After getting the name of the hotel and address, Kendra quickly offered, "I'm leaving my work now and will swing by my house and see you in about an hour. Is that okay?"

"It's more than okay. I'll make a reservation in the hotel's dining room for 6:30. I can't wait to see you again."

"Backatcha," Kendra replied, before adding a quick, "Bye."

Chapter 18

Kendra felt herself shaking as she entered the hotel's dining room. She was reminded of meeting Tim for the first time for breakfast in Texas. Even though she'd become comfortable with her appearance, and even though she felt comfortable with Tim; insecurities were still doing their best to surface. Whispering to herself, Kendra began to repeat the following words, "I am woman, and I can roar." Followed by, "You go girl, cuz you can do this."

Looking carefully down at her watch, the time was 6:35 . . . not too early and not too late. Although nervous, Kendra smiled at the hostess before saying, "I'm here to meet Timothy Blevins. Has he already been seated?"

After reaching for menus and nodding, she answered, "Please follow me."

Attempting not to obviously look for Tim—Kendra peeked carefully around the hostess until spotting Tim when he stood behind a table located next to a window. Kendra quickly thanked the hostess and held out her hand to Tim.

"After traveling all this way, I don't even get a hug," he asked with a pathetic frown."

"You're still being silly," she said.

"No I'm not. I'm being serious."

"All right . . . if you insist," she said, before moving directly in front of him.

Kendra expected Tim to gently give her a friendly hug but instead, he held her tightly and closely. As Tim was much taller, he needed to bend over until the sides of their heads met. For Kendra, the feeling was almost hypnotic . . . especially when breathing in his cologne."

When he released her, Tim exclaimed, "Gosh . . . that felt good. Did I tell you how much I've missed you? As my father would say, 'I've been hankerin' to do that for some time.'"

Without addressing his words, Kendra answered, "Thank you so much for flying here."

"Let me help you with your chair. By the way, I really like your perfume. It reminds me of visiting the Lilac Festival in Rochester, New York," Tim offered when she was settled.

"I'm glad you like it, but how does a guy from Uvalde, Texas visit Rochester, New York?"

Before Tim could answer, the waiter approached the table . . . asking, "Can I bring you something to drink or perhaps an appetizer."

Tim looked toward Kendra . . . receiving no answer, so said, "We haven't looked at the menu yet, but I'd like a beer on draft . . . whatever you have that's dark. You can surprise me." After taking Tim's order, the waiter turned and asked Kendra, "What can I get for you to drink?"

"I'll have a vodka and orange juice. I've forgotten what it's called," she answered.

"Do you have a preference of vodka for your screwdriver?" the waiter asked.

Mindful of the waiter helping her with the drink name, she answered shyly, "No, just vodka."

As soon as the waiter departed, Kendra asked again, "So how did visiting Rochester, New York come about?"

"I went to law school at Cornell University in New York. My roommate was from Rochester and invited me back to his home during Lilac Festival weekend. I'm thinking it must have been in May before we graduated in June."

"That's very interesting. So, did you also go to college in New York?"

"No, I went to college at the University of Houston. That's also where my father went to college. I planned to go to law school in Texas too, but received a scholarship to Cornell."

Their conversation was paused when the waiter returned with their drinks. Kendra said, "Thank you," while Tim said, "We'll order an appetizer in a few minutes."

After the waiter departed, Tim asked Kendra, "Is that okay with you?"

"Of course it is, but it seems like a good idea to look at the menu first before we order."

After opening the menu to the appetizer section and carefully perusing the full page of interesting items, Kendra placed the bulky menu down before saying, "Help . . . too many choices. I know you must be hungry . . . unless you cheated while waiting for me."

"That's not my style, I don't believe in cheating," Tim answered with a wink.

Not knowing exactly how to respond to Tim's odd remark, Kendra looked again at the menu.

After a brief pause, Tim asked, "Have you ever tried fried zucchini?"

"Are you talking about zucchini squash that's been fried?"

"Yes, it's one of my favorites."

"No but I'd like to give it a try. I've been branching out and trying new things lately, and it's been fun."

After waving to their waiter and ordering the appetizer, Tim said, "We'll order our meal when you bring our appetizer."

Kendra felt relaxed and marveled at how much that same secure feeling surrounded her each time she was with

Tim. She liked his manner of being in control but in a nice way. She thought about beginning with the questions she'd brought—folded carefully inside her purse—but for the moment, she was just enjoying his company and getting to learn more about him. Hopefully, he'd talk about his personal life before they got down to business.

While preparing her thoughts surrounding questions to ask Tim about his life with his parents, Kendra watched him take a big swig of beer. Opening her mouth to ask what his earliest memory of growing up was, Tim reached across the table and took her hand and said, "I want you to talk about yourself, so I can learn about your likes and dislikes." Then grinning, he asked, "What sounds good to you for dinner . . . what do you like to eat?"

"Really . . . cuz I'd like to know how you stay in such good shape while fixating on eating."

"That's interesting, since I asked you first about what sounded good to you for dinner."

"Hey, I don't know a lot about you, but I do know you like to eat."

"Okay, I'm busted. So, let's get the meal out-of-the-way, so we can talk about you."

"Yes sir. I actually already saw what I wanted, and I'll order it myself when it's time."

"Me too, so tell me about you while we wait to order."

Kendra took in a deep breath, wondering how much to share. She also wondered how much Tim already knew. Since there was really nothing good to know, an abundance of bad, and one really ugly incident, Kendra stared directly at him before seriously saying. "First, tell me what you already know about me."

"Actually . . . very little. My father was fairly vague but did say you'd been given the best of everything money could buy but still didn't have a happy childhood . . . or life. When I seemed confused, he told me, 'She'll share or not share her life . . . when she's ready.'"

"My life until lately has been very boring. I spent most of my young life attending all girl boarding schools. My senior year of college, I went with a tour group to Europe. That was the high-light of my life before starting to work. It was so interesting to see different cultures and how they lived. Bottom line—like I mentioned before—pretty boring. To be perfectly honest, I'd rather hear about you and your life.

As Tim began to talk about his life and being an only child, their appetizer arrived. After placing the appetizer between them, both ordered their entrees. Kendra ordered a chicken and avocado salad while Tim ordered a rib steak, a baked potato, and mixed vegetables. Before the waiter left and to Tim's surprise, Kendra asked for another screwdriver.

"I think you're having a good time," Tim remarked.

"I'm having a great time, and that's thanks to you."

Before Tim could comment, Kendra boldly said, "I'd like to make a toast. I'm not much on what's proper and what isn't so would that be okay?"

"Honey, nothing is off-limits between us. It's all about you enjoying yourself and doing what makes you happy."

"Okay, here goes. Thank you Tim for all you've done to help me. Thank you for helping me have a good time.

Above all, thank you for making me happy." Finishing, she added, "Sorry, I think I just made three toasts instead of one."

As they clicked glasses, Tim said, "It's been my pleasure. I'd like to keep making you happy long after the trust is completed."

Taken aback, Kendra asked, "Why?"

"Because you are special, and making you happy . . . makes me happy."

"That's sweet, but I'm definitely not special. I barely know who I am. I've basically been alone my whole life. My mother never even told me who I am, or even who I'm related to."

Before Tim could answer, their meal arrived. Their conversation was light . . . discussing the differences in their meal choices and how everything tasted so good. They even shared bites. It seemed to make Tim happy that Kendra liked the fried zucchini. When asked if they wanted dessert, both declined . . . surprising Kendra. She even asked, "Are you sure?"

As Tim asked for the check, Kendra watched him sign the credit slip. It went through her mind that Tim could be adding their meal charges onto a billing that would eventually come out of the trust. Did she care . . . absolutely not! However, that particular thought brought her back to the original reason for meeting Tim in the first place. However, the problem was—thinking of discussing business would somehow ruin the mood of the evening—going from light and fun to returning to her mother's devastating past and hers. It seemed too late now to start asking questions. Wouldn't it be better to meet again tomorrow and have a fresh discussion? Did Tim plan to stay another day or what? Should she pull the sheet of questions out or ask to go over the trust tomorrow? Continuing with her inner conversation, she couldn't believe how strange it was to want immediate answers before seeing Tim but now wanting to wait another day.

Instead of asking for Tim's plans, Kendra said, "It seems like whenever we're together, I'm always thanking you. So, here I go again. Thank you for the lovely dinner and asking me to join you."

As if Tim was reading her mind, he said, "We talked a lot about each other, but we didn't address any of your questions. Since we've both had a busy day, would you like to meet tomorrow? That way . . . we can also talk to my father?"

"I'd like that, but only if it doesn't mess up your plans. It will definitely help me find some closure to my past. Would you like to come to my place for lunch . . . say, about noon tomorrow?"

When Tim hesitated to answer, Kendra panicked before asking, "Are you leaving to go back to Texas early tomorrow? Will that be a problem?"

"No, but my father said he'd be going out on an afternoon boat—about noon—Texas time."

"So, that would be about ten o'clock my time . . . right?"

"How about 8:30 or 9:00 at your place? Since I'm all for being helpful . . . your words, I certainly want closure for you. Or, we could to it tomorrow evening? It's totally your choice."

"When do you need to return to Texas?"

"I have court Monday so fly back Sunday afternoon."

Proud of herself for easily making a choice, Kendra said, "Let's meet at my place . . . like about 8:30. I'll fix breakfast. I don't know how to fix grits, but I can make a mean omelet."

"Sounds good but please don't go to a lot of trouble."

When Kendra scooted her chair back, Tim said, "Hold on . . . let me help you up."

Standing, Kendra said with a grin, "Too late. I hate to leave, but we've both had a busy day." When she held out her hand, Tim grasped it like planning to shake it, but instead pulled her in against him, placed his hands on the sides of her head, and slowly . . . even gently, kissed her."

Kendra felt like she would surely melt away and slide to the floor. Feeling lightheaded and wanting to say how great that felt, she mumbled, "I better go."

"You don't have to . . . you know."

"Yes, I do. Besides, I've got things to do before tomorrow."

"Okay, if you insist, but let me walk you to your car."

* * *

After a busy first day at work, a delicious and very filling meal, and a couple of drinks, Kendra was hesitant to put off shopping until tomorrow . . . especially for an early breakfast.

Even after stopping to shop, placing the groceries away, changing into pajamas, and finally setting the alarm, she was unable to go to sleep. All she could think about was how much she liked Tim, and how wonderful the kiss felt. Although her emotions were hard to describe, she was now certain that her feelings were more than liking him. Unable to kid herself any longer, one thing she knew for sure; she had never felt this way about anyone before. Was this what love felt like, but how would she know? Was this enough of an emergency to call her therapist? Too late to call her now but maybe call after Tim left for Texas. As she drifted off, she continued to feel warm and fussy when remembering the feelings created by the unexpected kiss.

Chapter 19

It took Kendra a moment to realize the alarm was set to go off early for a reason. Tim was coming to breakfast, and she had lots of preparing to do. Dressing in a sweatsuit and laying out clothes for later; she thought how odd it was to have a guest—especially Tim—coming to her apartment. It was definitely a first . . . reminding herself of how many firsts she'd had lately.

Full of nervous energy, she'd barely had time to place the omelet ingredients in the refrigerator, take a shower, and dress before hearing the doorbell ring.

Hurriedly checking out her appearance in the entryway mirror, she opened the door and said, "Good morning and welcome."

From behind his back, Tim presented her with a bouquet of colorful mixed flowers. As Kendra took them and said, "How beautiful . . . thank you," she thought to herself . . . another first.

Watching Kendra take a moment to carefully look at the flowers, Tim asked with a grin, "Do the flowers make you happy?"

"They certainly do," she answered quickly. "Come on in."

Following Kendra inside, he offered, "Well, that was my hopeful wish."

Once Tim sat down, Kendra asked, "Can I get you a cup of coffee or tea?"

"Sure, a coffee would be nice, and black is fine."

"Since you're on a timeframe with your father, please let me know your wishes on how we should proceed," Kendra asked while handing Tim his coffee.

"Well, you know I'm always hungry," he answered with a grim.

"So, would it be okay to eat while we address some of my questions? As my mother often said in her notes, I've already got the fixin's ready."

"Can I do anything to help?" Tim asked seriously.

"No thanks," Kendra quickly replied. "I've got everything ready to go, but let's move to the dining room table. We'll have more room there. Is that okay?" Not waiting for Tim to answer, Kendra said, "I'll be right back."

When Kendra returned, she placed the flowers in the middle of the table and gave Tim a big smile. Before I start on the omelet, is there anything you do or don't want added to it, like a type of meat, vegetable, or hot items . . . jalapenos or stuff like that?"

"I know I'm from Texas and supposed to like hot foods, but—at best—I can only tolerate medium hot sauce."

"Okay, are you allergic to anything? Pausing for a moment for Tim's answer, Kendra exclaimed with a smile, "I don't want to poison you . . . at least not before you help with answers and go over the trust. While I'm preparing breakfast, let me give you the third letter. Would you mind to see if the trust is the same as the one you brought?"

"Sure, but I can help with breakfast. You know . . . I do a lot of cooking for myself."

"Well, you're probably better at it than I am, but I do make a lot of omelets. I'll call for help if I need you."

"Okay, but you can need me—even want me—even if you don't need help."

Looking momentarily perplexed, Kendra replied, "I think I understand what you just said, but I also think you're being silly again. We can still talk, cuz I can hear you from the kitchen." Feeling silly herself for having said that, Kendra quickly added, "I mean; the kitchen is obviously right next to where you're sitting." Mentioning the ability to hear him, Kendra was already planning to ask Tim some personal questions but didn't want him to see her facial expressions when hearing his answers . . . just in case they were answers she didn't want to hear.

Listening to sounds of the refrigerator door opening and closing and just after hearing pans clanking, Tim raised his voice when asking, "Can you hear me?"

"Loud and clear," she answered.

"I just opened the third letter and the trust is identical, but there is a small sealed letter inside the trust. I'll set it aside for you . . . okay?"

"Okay, thanks. Do you mind if I ask you a few personal questions?" Kendra asked.

"No . . . not at all. Unlike your life, my story is pretty much an open book."

"You're not married are you? I mean . . . like married but living separately."

"No, I'm not. But for full disclosure, I have been married one time before but now divorced."

"Do you have any children?" Kendra asked.

"No, we planned on getting settled first. We were only married a little over a year when my father had his first heart attack. I went to help him and returned early to find my wife in bed with one of the law partners where I worked. Hence, my earlier remark about being opposed to cheating."

Kendra rushed back into the dining room, saying, "Oh, my gosh! That's awful. I'm so sorry. However, you seemed to have handled it well and moved on. Good for you."

"Well, it wasn't meant to be. In the first place, I was never happy living in New York, but that's where she wanted to be. To make matters worse, her family always thought I didn't measure up to their standards. I was just starting out in the firm and as she told me before signing the divorce papers, 'I should have followed my parents' wishes and never married you.'"

Going back to the kitchen and taking a moment to ponder on Tim's disclosure, Kendra wondered what he knew about her past. Returning with placemats for the table, napkins, and utensils, Kendra declared, "Breakfast is almost ready. I'm just waiting on the biscuits."

"I would really like to help . . . please," Tim suggested again.

"Okay, you win. Follow me into the kitchen, and I'll put you to work," Kendra replied.

Arriving almost together, Kendra pointed to the kitchen counter opposite the stove before saying, "You can carry that tray of miscellaneous add-ons to the table. Maybe also pour yourself another cup of coffee. Oh, I forgot . . . I have a bottle of orange juice too . . . whichever you'd like or both."

"Wait a minute; I didn't say I'd come in here and do it all. And to verify, are you telling me that you didn't juice fresh oranges for me?"

"No, I didn't think I had time. Sorry!"

Shaking his head, Tim said, "Surely you don't think I'm serious. Guess you haven't gotten used to my sense of humor. I'm kidding for God's sake." Looking directly at her, Tim asked, "Why don't you come over here and give me a kiss, so I can say how sorry I am?"

Placing the spatula down after turning the omelet, she'd taken a tentative step toward him when the oven bell dinged. "Saved by the bell," Kendra said with a smile.

"Okay, but I'm due a kiss later," Tim replied quickly.

Opening the oven door, Kendra answered, "Maybe . . . that is . . . if you don't make anymore mean comments or complaints."

This time, it was Tim's turn to smile before saying, "Touché." While Tim carried the tray with preserves and butter for the biscuits and sour cream and a mild salsa—if wanted—for toppings on their omelets, Kendra followed closely behind with the basket of biscuits. Placing the basket on the table, Kendra said, "Oh, you still need your coffee cup filled. Would you like another cup or prefer a glass of not—emphasizing the word not—freshly squeezed orange juice?"

"I'm thinking the non-squeezed orange juice sounds perfect. Would you like a glass also?"

Receiving a quick nod from Kendra, Tim offered, "I'll fetch it from the kitchen."

"Okay, there are two glasses already out on the counter, and the juice is in the refrigerator. While you're getting our juice, I'll dish up the omelets."

Taking his first bite, Tim said, "I can honestly say this is absolutely the best omelet I've ever eaten. I can't think of a single item that would make it better. I've had lots of omelets in my lifetime, but none come even close to this one. This is so delicious."

"Well, that makes me happy . . . just like the flowers. If you want more omelet, there's still some left warming in the kitchen."

After clearing the table—Tim helped without being asked—Kendra said, "Let's put the basic perishable items away in the refrigerator. I'll clean the rest up after we talk. I certainly don't want to miss talking to your father . . . just in case . . . okay?"

"Sounds like a plan," Tim answered quickly.

"Can we sit at the table, so I can take notes?" With a nod from Tim, Kendra got out her list and a pen. "Okay, here goes. Is Charles W. Clayborne III my father?"

"Yes."

"Is he the person who set up the trust?"

"Yes."

"So, he's the person my mother referred to in her notes as Chuck?"

"Yes."

"So, was he a ranch hand when he helped my mother?"

"No. . . not even close."

"I finally came to that conclusion so looked him up and his company on the internet."

"Even back then, he was well on his way to running a large section of Texas land," Tim said.

"Was he married with two children already when I was born?"

"Yes."

"Shaking her head from side to side, Kendra asked, "But why? Why would he do that?"

"I can only tell you the basics, but Daddy knows more about the details. So, it's my understanding that Clayborne wanted your mother to abort you. When your mother refused, he eventually took her to San Antonio to give birth to you. I'm not sure when he told her that he was married, whether before or after your birth."

"Why did he lead her on like that? I mean . . . ask Mother to marry him, give her an expensive engagement ring, and tell her all of those lies. That makes no sense to me."

While shaking his head, Tim replied, "Now that your mother is gone; I think Clayborne will be the only person who knows those answers." Looking directly at Kendra, Tim followed with, "So, your mother never mentioned anything about . . . well, anything about that time in her life?"

"No . . . never! I just can't accept that anyone could be that cruel. After reading her notes, he was my mother's whole life."

"It doesn't make any sense to me either . . . really bazaar. Do you want to look at the trust before you talk to my daddy?"

"Yes, I guess so. I'd already figured out a lot of this but now faced with it . . . it's worse than I'd imagined. Glancing down through the remaining questions on the sheet, most of the ones left were when and why questions that Kendra didn't think Tim could answer . . . like: when or why did Clayborne initiate the trust?"

"Before we start on the trust, would you point out the bathroom to me?" Tim asked.

As Tim stood, his phone went off. Checking it out, he said, "It's my daddy."

Watching Tim walk down the hall, Kendra could hear some of the conversation, but not enough to know exactly what was being said. When Tim returned, he was no longer on the phone. Naturally, Kendra looked at him questionably before asking, "Is there a problem?"

"Well . . . yes and no. Due to a storm coming in, he's going out on a different boat and is leaving in a few minutes. He said he'd call when he gets back, asking me to tell you he's sorry."

Please tell me the truth and please be totally honest with me. You don't think your father is avoiding talking to me . . . do you?" Kendra asked hesitantly.

"Absolutely not! His exact words and I'll clean them up a little, 'All an old man wants to do is go fishin' and the gall darn weather is crapping on me.' He'll call for sure when he gets back. Remember, he's a couple of hours ahead of us. I'll stay until you're satisfied with knowing what transpired. Not that answers can ever be satisfying in your situation, and what you've lived through. Well, you know what I mean."

Taking in a deep breath, Kendra said flatly, "Okay, I'm ready to tackle the trust. I'll set the letter aside to read after finishing with the trust."

"Kendra, before we begin, I need to clarify something for you. Your mother's last name was never Smith. In actuality her last name was Taylor. She changed her name when she ran away from home. So, she is listed in the trust as Christine Smith, nee Taylor."

"It just keeps getting better and better," Kendra said sarcastically before asking, "What about me? Is my name really Smith?"

"Yes, your mother had the right to name you at birth . . . thus Smith is your legal name on your birth certificate."

"Thank you for preparing me for that. I would have been totally confused. Is there anything else I should know before we begin?"

"I don't think so, but be sure and stop me anytime you need any explanation. I hope going over the facts of the trust will bring you some sort of closure. I had to stop a couple of times myself to decipher your age and even your mother's age while reading the trust. I'll also tell you anything I can remember from what my father shared with me while reading through the trust."

Preparing herself for the worst, Kendra said, "Okay, let's start."

The first part of the trust sounded pretty basic, giving an overview of several terms used throughout the trust . . . what was binding and what wasn't. Kendra was more anxious to get to the meat of the trust and was getting impatient to move on. "Is this really what's important for me to know?" she asked.

"No . . . not really. This section is pretty much boilerplate. I'm just trying to be thorough. Actually, the trust is fairly small compared to today's standards. Moving right along, we're almost at the end of the first part of three. You'll definitely be more interested in the next two parts. Here's a little insight into why Charles Clayborne came to see my father . . . ah, asking him to draw up the trust in the first place. These are my daddy's words, 'Clayborne told me straight upfront that he wanted a no-body attorney to draw up the trust, and no one—his company's legal department, his family, or not another single person—could ever have access to the trust or know about it.' Father told me that Clayborne didn't come right out and threaten him but gave him the impression that there would be hell to pay if that ever happened. He visited Father twice . . . once to tell him what he wanted written into the trust, and secondly, when he signed it. I'll try to shorten the constantly used legal terms and the full names in order to speed it up for you. Okay, here goes with the next section."

As Tim turned to the page to the next section . . . separated by a sticky note, Kendra sat motionless, listening with her arms folded across her chest.

"Kendra Smith is named beneficiary of the trust, but because she is a minor, her mother, Christine Smith, nee Taylor—sorry, forgot to shorten—is considered her legal guardian. The funds are to be disbursed only for the benefit of Kendra Smith. Christine Smith will submit a recap on a yearly basis of exactly how monies had been spent during the year until her daughter reaches the age of twenty-six years old.

"John T. Blevins is named as trustee of the trust and will be responsible for administering any and all disbursements. If Kendra predeceases her mother in death, all funds will cease immediately."

Tim stopped reading and said, "I asked Dad what would have happened if he passed on before Christine or Kendra did? He'd told me that he'd asked Clayborne the same thing and had received a nonchalant shrug."

Before continuing, Tim asked Kendra, "How are you doing?"

"I'm okay . . . just want to get this over with."

"I understand," Tim answered before reaching over and patting her arm. "Here are the various stipulations listed with notice that if any are broken, all monetary settlements to the beneficiary and or guardian would immediately cease. To me . . . some seem not specific enough, but Father said that Clayborne gave him the list and wanted them listed just as he had written them."

- Christine Smith is to leave Texas and never return

- Trust will cover only necessary expenses for Kendra Smith until age twenty-six

- Trust will cover any and all schooling through college and additional advanced studies

- Any remaining assets or funds acquired by Christine Smith will go directly to daughter (Kendra Smith) upon her death

- Under no circumstances can Christine Smith divulge the name of her daughter's father or any information related to the father to any other person, including her daughter. If so, payments will immediately cease

- The trustee will oversee and manage the trust according to the legal declarations named within this trust

- The trustee will receive a flat fee of 1% of the remaining funds left in the trust account per the end of each calendar year in order to administer the trust and only when services are rendered during each calendar year, keeping a ledger accordingly

- The house near Sabinal, Texas—(the house only) and not the land below the house (see the attached deed)—is deeded to Christine but can be transferred to Kendra Smith upon Christine Smith's death.

- If Christine Smith marries, all trust payment will immediately cease.

Stopping, Tim looked over at Kendra before asking, "Are you still doing okay?"

"I don't really understand it. I mean . . . I hear the words but still have questions. Why did he give the house to Mother if she wasn't allowed to go back to Texas?"

"That would be another question for my father. I've noticed that you've been doing some off-and-on writing while listening."

"Yes . . . you're right. I'm adding questions for your father. Is the trust finished?'

"Almost, except for the last section . . . the funding page and signatures."

"So that part should say how much Clayborne gave Mother or me besides the house?"

"Yes, exactly," Tim answered flatly. Pausing to turn the page, Tim began again, "The original amount was a one-time amount of five hundred thousand. When you think about it, that was a pretty hefty amount back in those days. According to the signing date, you were almost two years old then. Too bad you were so young, or you could have shined some light on what was transpiring during that period. I take that back; it would have been a terrible time for you and your mother."

"Oddly enough, when I was in that old house, I had a strange feeling of being on the stairs before . . . the ones leading to the attic. I don't know if you remember, but there was a highchair in the attic. It must have been used by me . . . right?"

"That's weird, cuz according to my father and the dates on the trust; you were definitely there at that time. He even remembers seeing you as a very young child."

"Now I'm wondering why Mother stayed that long, because her notes made it seem like she had to leave when she returned from the hospital. I guess it really doesn't matter now."

Without saying anything to Tim, Kendra could hardly wait to ask his father what happened between the time she was born and when her mother left Texas. Maybe the unread sealed letter would help explain her mother's reasons and actions, and she wouldn't need to ask Tim's father for explanations. Whatever the reasons, her mother had made both of their lives miserable through the years. When she looked over at Tim, she was feeling totally numb.

Chapter 20

While opening her mother's final letter, Kendra asked Tim, "What more could Mother say to me? She's already apologized. I'm still trying to understand why she's been apologizing after all these years. She's had thirty years to explain her actions to me, to be honest with me, and say sorry. If she hadn't died suddenly, I wouldn't have learned the truth. Well, most of the truth . . . that is. In reality Mother has never told me exactly what she's been apologizing for . . . just constantly saying she's sorry and wants forgiveness. I'm being redundant, but I just don't understand. If I hadn't gone to see a therapist, I wouldn't have discovered myself or how to deal with my life."

"I didn't know you've been seeing a therapist. Would you like to talk about it?" After a momentary pause, Tim said, "I'm thinking your visits dealt with the loss of your mother?"

As she answered, "Yes and no but maybe later," Kendra wished she hadn't mentioned seeing a therapist. Immediately wanting to change the subject, she asked, "You've talked a lot about your father but haven't said anything about your mother."

As Tim discussed his mother's passing from cancer—happening while a senior in high school—his eyes began to water. "Sorry . . . sometimes it hits me like yesterday. It's been years, and I know it's not fresh like your mom's passing, but it brings back a lot of wonderful memories until she got sick. My father and I were holding her hands and talking about the fun things we'd done together. She was in and out of consciousness—because of the morphine for pain—but right before she passed; she squeezed my daddy's hand and smiled. I thought she smiled to let us know she was listening to our stories, but Father thought she smiled because she saw the light of heaven. I became a bitter and angry person, refusing to go to church after the funeral."

"I had no idea and shouldn't have brought it up, but I'm glad you have those wonderful memories to hold onto. I can't remember a single happy memory connected to my mother."

"No, it's perfectly okay and never a problem to talk to me about anything. Whenever I get frustrated or feel defeated, I remember what Mom told me when I was playing sports. 'Do the best you can do, and then you'll have no regrets. What's done is done and can't be changed, but not necessarily forgotten for the next challenge.' I fall back on her words more often than not."

"Did you ever return to church?" Kendra asked.

"Eventually . . . but not regularly," answered with a shrug. I'm still at odds with why she had to die. She was such a good and kind person. After the funeral, Daddy made a point to continue to go to church without me, and he still does. He often tells me that the anger will fade in time but that the love will endure forever."

Seeming to understand, Kendra said quietly, "Even though I was placed in many Catholic schools and was made to pray a lot, my mother told me that praying was a waste of my time and would never help anyone."

With her fingers shaking, Kendra carefully unfolded the letter and began reading out loud.

Dear Kendra,

I hope by now that you know all about what happened before I took you to California. I acted in such a stupid manner, and because of my stupidity; you suffered. Mr. Blevins helped me get what was best for our future. If I had not agreed to the trust, we would have been left with nothing. I was bitter and so disillusioned and blamed you for everything. As the years went by, I often thought that you would have been better off if I'd adopted you out. I lived a miserable life and placed you in a similar situation. I was too cowardly to tell you the truth . . . worried that you'd figure out who your father was, and do something to make us lose the money.

I placed the dead rose—the rose given to me with the engagement ring—in the trunk with my notes as a way of burying my dreams and life away. I had planned to bury the trunk but was hurried away before I could. The ground was very hard and even though I tried to stay longer, it wasn't meant to be. I did stay as long as I possibly could by saying you were ill or I was ill and couldn't travel . . . all the time hoping that somehow your father would leave his wife and make an honest woman out of me.

I can never take back the hurt you suffered at my hands, but I hope—for your sake—you can forgive me. Mr.

Blevins can help you with any questions that you may still have. I truly loved your father with all my heart and will until the day I die. I cannot understand why he acted as he did. I hope you'll be able to find happiness in your life. Happiness comes in many forms . . . none of which I was able to give you. Again, I am sincerely sorry.

Your mother, Christine Taylor

"What . . . not even signed "love mother," popped out. Feeling tears beginning to gather, Kendra didn't want to look over at Tim. She continued to stay still and look downward at the letter, not noticing that Tim had quietly walked around the table in her direction and was standing behind her chair. When he gently patted her on the shoulder and motioned for her to stand, she was startled and brought back to the present. Slowly standing and noticing his out-stretched arms, Kendra all but fell against him before bursting into tears . . . blubbering against his chest like a small child.

"Once I talk to your father, I'll finally be able to put this all behind me," she mumbled.

"Almost but not quite," Tim replied. Pausing for a moment, he added, "You'll still need to finalize the trust and take possession of the remaining assets."

"I know the trust and house are important, but neither were ever my priorities."

"Well, neither were my priorities either, but you always were," Tim answered quietly.

"But . . . why?" Kendra asked hesitantly . . . finding his remark confusing.

"I'm really not sure how it happened so suddenly. You just struck me as someone I wanted to get to know better . . . even get close to and protect."

"That doesn't make any sense," Kendra replied in a mumbled tone . . . still against his chest.

Lifting Kendra's chin and looking directly into her watery eyes, Tim offered, "I'm going to collect on the kiss I'm due . . . the one from the kitchen." Before Kendra could reply, Tim gently and longingly kissed her. This time, her entire body melted into him without embarrassment.

Finally pulling away, Kendra asked, "What should we do now until your father calls?"

"I've got a great idea. I'm hungry," he answered with a twinkle in his eyes.

"Are you serious? It hasn't been that long since we had a huge breakfast."

"I'm not hungry for food. I'm hungry for you. It's been a long time for me."

"Let's please go sit down and talk . . . maybe on the couch," was Kendra's immediate reply.

Sitting beside each other, Tim took Kendra's hand before saying, "Okay, I'm listening." Then, cocking his head to the side, he asked, "You're not gay . . . are you?"

"First, to answer your question . . . no, I'm not gay. However, I have never been with anyone before. I've thought about it . . . a lot and wondered what it would be like, but I'm petrified of disappointing you. You've made me happy in so many ways. So disappointing you would be the last thing I'd want to do. Please don't hate me for trying to explain my hesitancy."

"Surely, you don't think I could ever hate you. I've loved you for a long time . . . even from our first meeting. I haven't wanted to press you for personal information . . . heeding my daddy's words of waiting for you to share."

"Basically, I've lived my whole life alone and never knowing anything about my family history. If you'll notice, there are no family pictures on my walls, no mementoes of family trips, and forget about a Christmas tree or presents at Christmastime. I've recently branched out of my comfort zone by changing my daily routine but still feel vulnerable in so many areas. After reading about my mother's early life and my time while living with her, I'm afraid of ending up like her. I want to give my whole heart and soul to a man, but what if I end up a bitter person like she was. There's so much about my life that I'm ashamed to talk about. I've never had girlfriends to talk to. I've never had anyone to bounce ideas or thoughts off of. My therapist has been the only person in my entire life that I've been able to discuss my deepest secrets with."

"Do you mind telling me what she thinks you should do moving forward?"

Kendra answered quickly . . . almost like she was remembering the therapist's remarks word-for-word. "She always encourages me to follow my heart. When I told her that I wasn't sure what love felt like, she told me it would be like when I'd discovered myself, and I'd already accomplished that. Like, I'd know when it happened and just needed the courage to act on it."

Thinking about something else her therapist told her but didn't offer to tell Tim, "With every ending comes a chance at a new beginning so make the most of it, because chances are often fleeting." Looking directly into Tim's eyes, Kendra leaned over and kissed him before saying, "Follow me."

Leading Tim to the bedroom, Kendra walked over to close the bedroom blinds. When she began to unbutton her blouse, and even though her hands were shaking; she was not afraid.

Chapter 21

Hearing her phone ring, Kendra carefully scooted away from Tim, reached for her robe, and rushed to the dining room, wanting to grab the phone before the ringing disturbed Tim. When she looked at the number, she was surprised to see the call was from John Blevins. Finding it strange that he would call her instead of Tim, Kendra hesitantly answered, "Hello, Mr. Blevins. Is everything okay?"

"Couldn't be better . . . caught a boatload of fish today—no pun intended—in spite of the rough weather. I called my son's phone several times, but it kept sending me to voice mail. But that's fine, cuz now I can apologize directly to you for taking much too long to personally speak with you."

"That's all right. I've been taken real good care of by Tim," she replied. Grinning to herself, Kendra thought . . . if he only knew!

As John Blevins continued to speak, Kendra quickly made her way back to the bedroom and Tim. While on her way and trying to stall, she said, "I'm sorry, Mr. Blevins; I didn't quite hear what you just said."

"It's probably our connection. I was asking if you wanted to start asking me anything. Tim told me you were keeping a list of questions."

"Yes, definitely! Would you hang on a moment, so I can get my list?"

"Sure, Honey . . . take your time."

Knowing her list was in plain sight on the dining room table, Kendra entered the bedroom and called Tim's name. With no answer, she gently patted him on the shoulder and watched him stretch before slowly opening his eyes. "Well, hello Sweetheart. Do you want to get back in bed with me?" Tim asked with a sleepy grin.

"No, I need to tell you something," Kendra answered quickly.

"Was it that bad?" Tim asked, while reaching for her.

Backing away and answering in a rushed manner, "Your father is on the phone."

"On the phone right now or called?" Tim asked sleepily.

"Yes, on the phone now. He tried to call you several times but got your voice mail so called my phone."

"Do you want me in on the conversation?" Tim asked seriously.

"Yes . . . please. I'm supposed to be getting my list of questions, so you need to hurry."

Without waiting for Tim's response, Kendra hurried back to the dining room before saying, "Okay, I'm back. I'm going to place you on speaker . . . if that's okay, so Tim can join into our conversation."

"Of course," was quickly replied.

Hoping Tim would be in the room soon, Kendra offered, "Thank you again for calling to answer my lingering questions. Even after reading Mother's notes, reading her letters, and seeing the trust, I hope you'll be able to fill in the remaining unknowns for me."

"Well, I'll do my best. I'm at your service . . . Little Lady."

"Uh, here's Tim."

"Hi Daddy," Tim chimed in.

"Hi Son," was answered just before saying, "I'm glad you gave me Kendra's phone number. You need to check your phone more often," was added with a tad of sarcasm."

"Sorry, it's been on the charger. How'd the change in boat service go . . . catch a bunch of fish?"

"It went great! I'll use them again next time."

"Hopefully, next time will be in several months from now," Tim answered forcefully.

"Maybe or maybe not that long. I'm again thinking seriously about retiring. Retirement is becoming more and more appealing. I've realized I'm not good at sticking to schedules or meeting deadlines anymore, and fishing is definitely where I belong. Well, that's a discussion for another time. We'll talk more about that when I get back. Okay, Kendra, are you ready?"

"Yes, Sir . . . here goes. I just finished reading Mother's last letter . . . ah, the one found inside the trust. It wasn't dated. My question is . . . do you remember when you received it?"

"Now, let me think. It was after your twenty-sixth birthday, and you'd moved out on your own. She had already sent the others to me . . . specifically asking that I keep that particular letter inside her copy of the trust and to keep everything together for you until she passed. So, the short and long of the answer is approximately four or so years ago."

"Hum . . . interesting. So, going back to reading Mother's notes, who originally owned the old house where the trunk full of notes was found?"

"The house was built and owned by the original purchasers of the land. That would be your father's grand-parents. They lived in the house several years before moving and building another house on a different section of land . . . much nicer and more convenient to town. Seems like his grandmother didn't like living where there was little access to necessities for her children. Your father's parents . . . ah, your grandparents, eventually built an estate in San Antonio . . . complete with horse breeding stables. As they became older, they eventually moved to Austin. I'm thinking your father and his immediate family presently live in both houses. No one has ever lived in your mother's house since she left. I'm thinking you were around two years old then.

"How do you know all this? I mean . . . where did you find this information?" Kendra asked.

"It's a no-brainer round these here parts . . . Texas that is. The beginning of the Clayborne dynasty is well-known; not only for their cattle production but also for their oil holdings."

"Okay, I get the picture but what I don't understand is why the house was deeded to my mother and eventually to me?"

"When your mother lived there, she pretty much considered it her house . . . or was convinced it would be hers as soon as she and your father married. Clayborne basically gave it to her but not the land . . . sorta as a peace offering. He told her that she had to leave Texas, and that he was having the house bulldozed. Knowing how much she felt attached to the house, he told her that if she agreed to the stipulations in the trust and would leave without creating a fuss or making trouble for him; he'd not destroy it. Once she agreed; he promised to give the house to her. She told me that she'd only agreed in order to keep the trunk there and a few other items that were impossible to take with her on the airplane. She also told me—very proudly—that she'd never owned anything in her whole life . . . much less her very own house."

"The house is in such terrible condition—even dangerous—and the rat-infested boxes were beyond disgusting," Kendra offered.

"I know . . . Tim told me."

"I was going to ask you why she waited two years or so to leave, but she pretty well explained all that in her final letter. Regardless for how she felt about the house; I'm now wondering what I should do with it?"

"I've given that question a lot of thought myself. It would be expensive to demolish the house due to its location. I know of nothing there worth salvaging, and I can't see anyone wanting to purchase it. On face-value, it's basically worthless. Having said that, I'd say . . . just let it be. Once the deed is placed in your name, it's legally yours. I'd recommend keeping the deed in a safe place for future reference. I'm thinking if something happened to it in the future, you would definitely have some sort of regress."

"Okay, thanks for your advice. Let's see . . . how did you send the reports to Clayborne? Can you explain what that process was like? I mean . . . did you personally communicate with him?"

"According to the terms of the trust, I did for the first few years. I mailed certified accounting information directly to him, but then he called and told me to stop sending it. He stated that he desired to distance himself from the circumstances and wanted no paper trail to trace back to him. Of course, I asked him to put his request in writing. I did, however, continued to keep all transactional records . . . just for my own protection. You are more than welcome to see the years of information at any time you wish. Since it's more or less the story of your life from a financial viewpoint, you might find it interesting."

"I mean no disrespect when I inquire about your fees and also . . . ah, is there any actual money left from the original trust amount?"

"No disrespect taken and again . . . absolutely no problem to ask me anything. I'm thinking you've got gumption to inquire. That's exactly the questions you should be asking. Yes, I did receive a fee for my services—according to the requirements of the trust—prudent only to maintaining the trust and necessary expenses. Yes, there is some money left. It belongs totally to you and is in an account presently drawing interest. I'm thinking there is about $50,000 in it. You can receive a full accounting whenever you please. Full disclosure . . . your mother requested a reverse mortgage on her house years ago and the property has already been taken back. Her car was totaled in the accident and the insurance money—which wasn't much—was placed into that same savings account."

"That's interesting. I hadn't even considered her house. It never meant anything to me."

"I understand," John Blevins answered rather matter-of-factly."

"Thank you so much for clearing some of this up for me. Do you mind if I ask you a personal question regarding my mother's relationship with Clayborne?"

"Of course not . . . ask away, and I'll answer if I can."

"Do you have any idea why he led my mother on . . . the despicable acts of lying to her, getting engaged when already married, sending her and me away . . . and the likes?"

"Like I said before; at the onset I only got involved to draw up the trust. I can tell you that he paced around the room for a bit before finally sitting down to address his reason for hiring me. He was saying how he got into a jam, and the predicament was way over his head. I can't remember his exact words but something like: how he felt sorry for this young girl in the beginning. He was mumbling, talking real fast, and hard to hear or understand. It was something about how his wife not only hated living in the country but also hated the cattle business, so she'd spent most of her time up north. He was obviously trying to justify what he'd done. He didn't come right out and say it, but I got the impression a divorce would ruin him and the family business financially. To be totally honest with you and knowing how hurtful this will sound, he wanted you and your mother out of his life without his wife or family getting even a whiff of impropriety. I was upfront with him . . . telling him that I was picked to provide a service and not to judge his actions. I did my best to follow his wishes while helping your mother as much as possible through the years. I helped her with purchasing her house in California, so you'd have a roof over your head."

"Do you know why the trust said she would lose everything if she married?"

"That was Clayborne's way of protecting himself. A husband would surely ask questions."

What is your suggestion on what I should do now?" Kendra asked hesitantly.

"I don't quite understand your question, Honey."

Before replying, Kendra looked in Tim's direction. Tim returned her look with raised eyebrows, also not understanding her question.

"Well, I'm not sure exactly how to proceed at this point. Do I just sign for the trust transfer and the bank account and leave it there?" Before receiving an answer, Kendra blurted out, "Shouldn't I confront Charles Clayborne for what he did?"

"Whoa . . . hold your horses. That's a question only you can decide. Have you thought this through? I'm talking about the pros and cons of doing that, and are you prepared to open that can of worms? What is your ultimate goal, and what do you want to gain from doing so?"

"Actually . . . I haven't thought about confronting him until now. I do know that he is presently running for Congress. I found that out on the internet. I sometimes think that he should be hurt like he hurt my mother. That hurt was also passed on to me through the years in so many subtle ways."

Having never mentioned Albert to Tim, Kendra couldn't help but wonder if John Blevins knew anything about what happened to her. She was certain that he knew everything about her until she moved out, but did he keep up with her after that? When she mentioned that her mother's California house meant nothing to her, she remembered his remark of, "I understand." Did he know how unhappy she'd been there? Maybe she'd find out at another time.

"Thank you, Mr. Blevins, for calling and for helping my mother and me through the years. I'll work out signing the documents with Tim. Perhaps we can meet soon in person."

"You're welcome, Honey. You take care now, and I certainly look forward to meeting you too."

"Bye for now," Kendra replied before disconnecting the call.

Looking in Tim's direction, Kendra smiled sexually before asking, "Are you still hungry?"

Chapter 22

Although knowing it was necessary for Tim to return to Texas, and even though she didn't want him to leave; Kendra was having a tough time accepting the inevitable. The last few days had been the happiest in her life, and she didn't want the joy, euphoria, exhilaration—or whatever she was experiencing—to end. Frankly put, she was more than beside herself over Tim's returning home. Her feelings had nothing to do with being by herself but more about saying goodbye and the possibility of never feeling his arms around her again. While contemplating his leaving, Kendra couldn't keep from wondering if her feelings were similar to how her mother felt each time Chuck left. Although knowing that comparing the past didn't make sense—because the circumstances and persons were so different—she still couldn't stop.

After seeing Tim off at the airport—even watching his plane take off—Kendra found herself depressed and wishing her therapist was available to give suggestions. She had another week before her scheduled visit but wished the appointment was sooner.

Her Sundays were usually spent preparing for work . . . laying out professional clothes to wear Monday and other routine preparations but not today. Her each and every moment was spent reflecting on her time with Tim . . . so many wonderful moments in so little time.

After Kendra told Tim of her willingness to sign the papers in front of a notary and forward everything to him, he'd suggested meeting again in Texas and handling it together. After explaining how she was starting a new job and had no vacation time to use, the disappointment on Tim's face was both unexpected and insightful . . . even amazing. Never in her entire life had anyone—especially her mother—shown any signs of disappointment about not seeing her again. As they'd shamelessly kissed goodbye at the airport, Kendra promised to ask for a three-day weekend as soon as possible. With a big smile, Tim promised to call when he arrived home but reminded her of the two hour time difference, the time spent on picking up his car from airport parking, and the time spent on the drive to Uvalde. Kendra met Tim's thoughtful reminders with watery eyes. Before assuring him that she would be waiting to hear from him regardless of the time and wouldn't rest until learning he'd arrived safely home, she told him, "I've gotten used to the two hour time difference, so I'm finally good with it."

While watching a late night movie, Kendra grabbed the phone even before the first ring finished and noticed it was 1:30 a.m. California time. When answering without saying hello, she inquired in a probing tone . . . yet forcefully, "Please tell me that you're home."

"Yes, I am but exhausted. I hoped to sleep on the plane but couldn't. Guess that's your fault, cuz I missed you so much. Since I have an early court date—Daddy's case—I better hit the sack. Now that's my daddy's fault, cuz he's still fishing somewhere in Mexico," said sarcastically.

"But as Daddy often says, 'I'm plum tuckered out.' Then, he sometimes follows up with, 'It's not like pickin' cotton in the noon day sun, so I shouldn't complain.' I'm sorry for going on and on. It must be the lack of sleep talking. So, how is everything going with you? Are you doing okay?"

"Yes, I'm fine . . . and even better now that you've called. Get some rest and call me when you get caught up." Not wanting to end the call but knowing she should, Kendra awkwardly blurted out, "Thank you for calling . . . love you . . . bye."

Feeling embarrassed and fearing what Tim's response might be, she immediately disconnected the phone. However, while placing the phone down, she received an immediate text that read, "I like it and love you too."

Staggering off to bed and having mixed emotions of giddiness and tiredness, she didn't need to see herself in the mirror to see the wide smile—bordering on silly—on her face.

As Kendra drove to work the following morning, she was already planning on how to ask for a three-day weekend off. She was willing to work extra each day in order to facilitate the time away and if necessary, work online while absent. Thinking how Tim's office was usually closed on Fridays, a Friday would be a better choice than a Monday. She planned to explain to management how important it was to legally complete her mother's estate and take possession of her mother's assets . . . noting the inconvenience but the necessity of traveling to Texas. She hoped they would understand and let her off as soon as possible.

Nothing ventured . . . nothing gained came to mind as she entered the front door at work. Not only that—but one way or another—she would see Tim as soon as she could . . . even if she had to quit. After all, she was in love and that was all that mattered.

Chapter 23

Hardly able to control her enthusiasm, Kendra walked hurriedly into the therapist's office. Even before sitting down, she offered, "Boy, am I glad you're back."

"Since you didn't contact me with an emergency, I'm guessing you've been doing fine."

"Better than fine . . . like great. So much has happened since you've been gone, and I've got lots to tell you. Can I start? Oh, I'm sorry . . . did you have a good time on your vacation?"

"Yes, I had an amazing time. It was the first time since beginning my practice to take a long vacation . . . usually just a few days here and there. I must admit that it took awhile to distance myself from my patients and concentrate only on myself and my family. Okay, that's enough about me. I want to talk about what's been happening with you."

"I hardly know where to begin, cuz I have so much to talk about. Let's see. After our last visit, I felt a lot better about confronting things. In the past, I've been intimidated by the unknowns of my life, but now I need help in dealing with what I presently know. Well, let me tell you what happened. The son of my mother's attorney . . . ah, Tim . . . I think I told you about his assistance when I was back in Texas . . . didn't I? I can't remember. Anyway, he flew out here to settle my mother's estate, because his father—Mother's original attorney—was fishing somewhere in Mexico. Tim's also an attorney. Did I tell you that?"

"Kendra . . . slow down, take a deep breath, and relax. We have plenty of time. There's no need for us to rush."

As Kendra took a deep breath and offered a grin, she realized she hadn't been taking deep breaths in quite some time . . . usually her coping mechanism when fearful about how to proceed.

After a short pause, she began again. "Well, by then, I'd finally finished reading through my mother's notes but still had questions. Tim was able to explain the trust and answer many of my questions but not all of them. Even though Mother's attorney was still fishing in Mexico, I was finally able to talk with him over the phone. He was helpful in answering more of my remaining questions. Naturally, a few of the questions about my mother's life before he was hired to do the trust weren't answered. It's hard to believe, but he remembered seeing me as a small child before I left Texas."

"So, you're pretty much finished with your mother's estate and now able to move along with your new and improved life?"

"Not exactly, cuz I'm now at several crossroads on how to proceed and need your help with making wise choices. I know you've always said that the choices are mine to make, but now I find myself stuck in foreign territory."

When the therapist frowned, Kendra giggled before saying, "I'm kidding."

"Well, how about that . . . my serious Kendra is actually kidding? How great is that. Good for you. I must admit that I initially thought you were contemplating leaving the country . . . perhaps moving to Mexico. A tad confused; I just wanted to hear more."

"Okay, let's see; what's next on my unwritten list to talk about? Did you notice that I didn't bring a list to refer to?"

"Well, as Frasier would say, 'I'm listening.'"

With a knowing grin and a nod, Kendra let the therapist know she understood the reference to an old television character. "Well, I'll be traveling to Texas in two weeks to finalize the paperwork. I'll get the Texas house—which is totally worthless—and the balance of the money in a trust saving account . . . about fifty thousand dollars. That's where the foreign territory comes into play. I could have finalized the trust from here but honestly wanted to see Tim again. Hence, Tim's my foreign territory . . . emotionally that is."

"Okay . . . do you want to elaborate?"

"Since Tim's one of my two current dilemmas, I'm hoping to get guidance from you. I have strong feelings for him. In fact, I think I'm in love with him. I'm not sure if I'm feeling true love or caught up in the moment of receiving attention . . . which I really like . . . by the way. He seems interested in me, but when I'm alone; I can't keep from asking myself why."

"Due to your past history, your hesitancy about how you feel is completely warranted. And, I must say that it's healthy for you to question your feelings. Have you done a list of the pros and cons?"

"Yes I have, but I'm finding it hard to be objective. The only negative I'm able to find is the distance between us . . . not emotionally but from California to Texas."

"Understood, but have you decided to sleep with him yet? That should give you a lot of insight into your relationship . . . especially after what happened to you . . . well, you know."

While embarrassed and knowing she must also appear embarrassed, Kendra looked down before mumbling, "Yes, we already did."

"Okay, and how did that go for you?" asked matter-of-factly without any outward reaction.

"It was wonderful, amazing, and incredible. Remember, you told me to follow my heart." Grinning, Kendra added, "To be perfectly honest, I don't think it was my heart beckoning."

"I can't tell you how impressed I am with you and your attitude. You go girl!"

"You know . . . before we slept together, I never thought about what happened with Albert. See, I can even say his name, and it's not a problem for me anymore."

"Does Tim know about the Albert debacle?"

"No, I don't think so. I haven't told him but often wonder if his father knows. Like . . . has his father kept tabs on me before and after my mother's passing? He definitely knew how to get in touch with me. Remember, I was in the hospital when Mother died in the car accident. If Tim's father does know about what happened to me, then I'm sure he's said something to Tim about it. When I told Tim I had a therapist appointment, he assumed it was because of Mother's passing. I'm thinking about letting it be for now. I know in my heart that what happened with Albert was not my fault, and I'm okay with it now. Perhaps sometime in the future—if we've made a life together—I'll share the experience with Tim."

"I agree with you. Let the past stay in the past. I believe our past history is only important as long as it doesn't keep us from moving forward in the present or into the future. So, after you slept together, did anything change with your relationship?" was asked in a serious manner.

"I think it did . . . and for the better. I think we're a lot closer now. That's how I feel, and I think Tim feels the same way. He didn't seem to want to leave for Texas after his visit, and I didn't want him to go either. It was weird, but I couldn't help but wonder if Mother felt the same way when she was with Chuck . . . ah, my father. That's my other dilemma I need your input on. Do we have more time before your next appointment arrives?"

"We're doing just fine . . . time wise. Again, I'm so happy about how well you're doing."

"Okay . . . good. After finishing Mother's notes, reading her apologies, and finding out who initiated the trust, I learned a lot about my father. He led her on and even gave her an engagement ring. Because of his lies, she was planning to marry him and have a happy future with him. Come to find out, he was already married and had two children. And, he wasn't a ranch hand but part of a wealthy family. When Mother became pregnant and had me, he sent us to California . . . telling her to never let me or anyone know that he was my father. If she did, then she would lose everything and the trust would be nullified. The money could only be used for my care, schooling, and the like. She could use the money to make sure I had a place to live. The trust was pretty straight forward. Even though she took her bitterness out on me, I've found myself feeling somewhat sorry for her."

"Wow, that's a lot to hear . . . even for me. Believe me; I've heard a lot of circumstances through the years. Kendra, you've actually come a long way in a fairly short time."

"I know what you're saying. Sometimes, I've caught myself finding it hard to believe too. I've tried to put myself in her shoes . . . being alone with a small child to feed and no money."

"Our time is almost up so is there anything else you want to discuss?"

"Well, I still want to hear your thoughts on how to proceed with Tim and my biological father. How do I handle Tim's and my relationship? I've heard that long distance romances very seldom work out. Secondly, how do I handle the situation with my father? The stipulations were only placed on Mother. Oh, I should also tell you—whether it matters or not—he is both rich and influential. He's running for Congress in Texas."

"Let me first talk about when you visit Tim in Texas. You can discuss how you feel about being apart, how you both feel about having a long distance relationship, and where you both want to imagine your futures."

"During my last conversation with Tim—soon after he returned to Texas—he talked about taking over his father's practice and moving the office to San Antonio . . . saying he had more connections there. He also said it would be a better place than Uvalde to raise a family."

"Really? How did you answer that rather leading remark?"

"I changed the subject. I went back to wondering how I should answer . . . unsure of where I really stood. This feeling of loving someone is a first for me. Part of my emotions constantly revisit how Mother loved a man who wasn't the person he pretended to be."

"This sounds like a novel of love and betrayal . . . maybe emotional and moral abandonment."

"I've often thought the same thing. It was almost like reading a mystery novel and finally learning the truth of why she was so secretive. Not that it takes away the years of being basically alone and ignored. Not knowing anything about my relatives . . . especially who my father was. What is your suggestion about . . . like, do you think I should look up my father and confront him?

"Kendra, I'm really sorry but it is time for our session to end."

"So, you're leaving me still up in the air about what to do about Charles Clayborne?" His actual name is Charles Wesley Clayborne . . . the third."

"Honestly, it's hard for me to suggest anything right now. This situation is totally new to me, and I need time to give it more thought. Whenever I give suggestions, it's always doing so with what I feel is best for you. Maybe you can do a little research and give me more particulars at our next session. Usually, we've been meeting once a month. Do you want to keep to our regular schedule?"

"I guess so, but I'll be going to Texas before then," Kendra answered hesitantly. Adding, "Tim and my father are both in Texas but thankfully not in the same town."

Before more conversation was given or received, the intercom beeped before saying, "Sorry to interrupt, but your next appointment is waiting."

Kendra stood quickly and quietly waved. As she turned to leave, she clearly heard the therapist say, "Kendra, I'm so proud of you. See you next month."

Entering the car, Kendra was in a puzzled state of mind. In the past—whenever leaving the therapist's office—she'd felt relieved or felt energized to go forward with her life . . . even uplifted on how to proceed. But for now, she'd focus on doing a good job at work and preparing for her time away. Starting the car, Kendra resolved to have no more thoughts about her father.

However, as she made her way home, Kendra couldn't help but wonder what Tim's opinion would be on whether or not she should seek out her father, whether or not she should confront him, or whether or not it would be best to just ignore him altogether? Since she already valued Tim's way of objectively approaching other situations, maybe he could help her with the best way forward regarding her father.

Thinking of being in Tim's arms again gave her an immediate warm and fuzzy feeling.

Chapter 24

While thinking about getting to the airport on time and flying to San Antonio, Kendra assured her team that she would be away for only a short amount of time . . . probably three work days at the most. As Kendra concluded the eleven o'clock staff meeting, she further explained, "Remember, if something comes up that you feel uncomfortable about handling, I'm only a phone call or e-mail away."

Leaving for work this morning, she'd already packed her suitcase and placed it in the car. This way, she'd have plenty of time to finish the team meeting, drive straight to the park and ride, and have someone take her the few blocks to the airport. Then, she'd be off to be with Tim.

As the flight landed on time and without a single problem, Kendra momentarily wondered if Tim would be as excited to see her as she would be to see him. During their last conversation, he'd told her, "Don't worry about anything and trust me to make all the necessary arrangements. I'll handle everything, while your job will be to relax and enjoy your time in Texas with me." True to his word, she could hardly control herself when she scanned the arrival gate and found Tim holding a sign that read: Welcome Kendra.

After a tightly held hug and lengthy kiss, Tim said, "Let's pick up your luggage. It's this way." Finding herself in unfamiliar surroundings and beginning to feel like wondering through a dream, Kendra was unable to find the right words to describe her happiness at actually being with Tim again. Instead of saying something about still learning how to handle first time experiences and unfamiliar situations, she smiled before saying, "Okay . . . let's do it. I'll follow you; lead on Macduff." Staying closely behind Tim, she saw a large sign with an arrow pointing to the Baggage Claim Area . . . thinking . . . guess I'm not lost after all. On their way and before arriving at the luggage carousel, Kendra mentioned that her suitcase would have a bow of red yarn on the handle. While waiting, Tim moved closely behind her, before leaning over and whispering into her ear, "I can't wait to be alone with you."

Once sitting comfortably in Tim's car, her suitcase and computer placed safely in the trunk, Kendra finally relaxed. Instead of telling her what their immediate plans were, Tim placed his hands on each side of her face and said, "I sure missed you," before longingly kissing her.

Looking directly into Tim's eyes, Kendra seriously replied, "I missed you more and love you with all my heart." When Tim seemed puzzled and didn't answer immediately, she dropped her eyes . . . feeling embarrassed . . . almost humiliated for offering up her innermost feelings.

"Please look up at me," Tim finally said. "I love you too. You've just said the words I've wanted to say to you for some time. I've been afraid of rushing you . . . concerned that you'd find me pushy or questioning my feelings were over the top . . . or too soon. I really can't explain my strong emotions for you, but I've been in love with you from the very first day we met. Although we haven't known each other very long, I've grown to love you more and more with each passing day. Daddy said you'd been through a lot in your fairly short life and not to rush you. He never explained or gave any details but said for me to be gentle with you. Whatever he was referring to; you can talk about it or not . . . now, anytime, or never. Please know that anything you could possibly tell me would never change my feelings for you."

"Now I understand; I really do and thank you for loving me. This will sound bazaar, but I've never felt loved before . . . ever. Okay, let's change the subject. Are you hungry?" Kendra asked with a grin and a glint in her eyes.

"Yes, I'm starved. So, are you talking about food?"

"No, are you?" Kendra answered with a big smile.

"Well, you better get prepared, cuz I've been starving since we were last together."

After a quick check-in at the hotel—not far from the airport and already pre-registered—they made love like wild animals. During each new sexual encounter, both seemed to learn and understand what pleased the other person. Both seemed happy about their sexual togetherness as well as their time together in general. Above all, Kendra felt safe, loved, and content with Tim.

Having already visited a doctor to procure birth control pills, Kendra felt fairly sure of not getting pregnant. But as she started taking them, she couldn't help but wonder how her mother became pregnant . . . especially since mentioning getting birth control pills in her notes. Did her mother stop taking the medication for some reason, did she get pregnant on purpose, or did she get pregnant in spite of taking the pills? Strangely, and even though she tried not the think about it, each time she swallowed a pill, thoughts of her mother becoming pregnant with her would return. Then, those thoughts would lead to how Mother considered her the reason for her life being ruined. Sometimes, after downing a pill, she would shudder.

Finishing her shower, Kendra hollered, "Tim, I'm really hungry . . . but for food this time. Do you have plans for us to eat?"

"Yes ma'am. I've already made dinner reservations for us in the hotel's dining room."

"That sounds perfect. I'm so hungry; I could eat a horse. Maybe that's because I recently had a strenuous work-out." Moving closer to where Tim was sitting, Kendra stopped to see if he got her reference to their love-making calisthenics. Receiving a smile from him, she continued, "Also, I only had a fruit smoothie for breakfast and no lunch."

"I made our dinner reservation here, because I didn't think you'd feel like going out after traveling. If you'd prefer to go somewhere else, I can easily cancel it."

When Kendra strutted by in front of him—wearing only a thong and no bra—Tim reached out and patted her gently on the fanny.

"Be careful or we'll need to stay in and order room service," Kendra quipped with a grin.

"We'll do whatever makes you happy," Tim answered playfully with raised eyebrows.

Sitting down on the bed next to him, Kendra asked, "Why is that? I really don't understand. You've always been so helpful and seemingly going out of your way to please me."

"Let's talk more about that at dinner, but the long and short of it is: because I want to please you, because I can, and because I love you."

"I like your answer, but I'd also like to talk more about your thoughts on the future . . . our future. I'll hurry and get ready."

Their conversation during the meal was light and informative as they both discussed different aspects of their jobs. Unable to pass up the restaurant's signature dessert, they split a large piece of decadent pecan pie topped with ice cream and drizzled with pecan syrup.

"I've had another perfect day with you," Kendra offered. "You always make me feel special, but I worry that I'll do or say something that might change that."

"What you see and the way I treat you is just me. I'm not perfect and have made lots of mistakes in my past. I married way too young and realized way too late that we weren't even close to being compatible. One thing I'll tell you from the bottom of my heart . . . I will never purposely hurt you. And for sure, I would never hurt you the way your father hurt your mother."

Deciding now was as good a time as any to delve into the questions that only Tim could answer. Kendra reached across the table and took Tim's hand before asking, "What do you see happening with us moving into the future," she asked seriously.

"Well, I think it's a given that we love each other. Having said that; my daddy is definitely retiring by the end of the year, so that means I only have three months to decide exactly where I want to practice. Like I said before, I'd like to move the practice to San Antonio. Daddy doesn't care where I take the firm as long as I do my best to service his present clients. I've already told him not to be concerned about that, because I'll always do my best for them."

Cocking her head to the side, Kendra asked, "So, if you move the firm to San Antonio, what are your thoughts or plans about me being in California and you being in Texas?"

"I've already given that scenario a lot of thought. Maybe before I answer your question, how would you feel about relocating to San Antonio? Would you be interested in doing that? Would that be possible? Have you even thought about moving?"

"Slow down cowboy! Our give and take questions are reminding me of my last session with my therapist."

When Tim quickly asked, "And, how did that go?" While caught off-guard by his question, Kendra wasn't sure if he was being flippant or serious.

"Have you ever been to a therapist before?" Kendra inquired. Not waiting for his answer, she continued, "That's exactly—almost word for word—what a therapist would ask. Sometimes, they'll ask, 'And, how did that make you feel?'"

"Actually . . . yes, I have. My ex-wife and I attended a couple of pre-divorce sessions. I don't remember the therapist saying anything like you just mentioned. She mainly concentrated on us being young and having different out-looks on our futures. So . . . let's get back to how you feel about our distance situation."

"Well, let's see. I did discuss how strong my feelings were for you, but that you lived in another state. She reminded me that at this point in my life, the choices I make are mine alone to make and not to run from them. My therapist is a big believer that people who are partners should make decisions together . . . like having the same goals and wishes moving forward. Because of my mother's secrecy, I was never able to discuss anything with her. Basically, my therapist has been like a trusted family member to me. Luckily, I've been able to discuss anything with her without holding back. Since Mother constantly told me what to wear, how to act, where to go, what to do, and what not to do, I basically lived my whole life without making any choices on my own . . . absolutely none. In fact, my choices began with Mother's passing."

"So, what is your choice about staying in California or moving to San Antonio?" Tim asked.

"I guess my choice would depend on you," Kendra answered in a cautious manner.

"That doesn't quite answer my question . . . does it? How about this, and I'll cut right to the chase. What do you want? Would you be willing to relocate to San Antonio to be with me?"

"Well, about that. I've given a lot of thought about moving to Texas, and at this point in my life; there's nothing I can think of that would make me happier. For sure, there's nothing holding me back. So, if I cut right to the chase, my choice and answer would be . . . definitely yes. I'll admit that I am both frightened and excited at the same time. Naturally, my move will be much easier than yours. I'll only have a few loose ends to deal with in California—nothing permanent or family to deal with—just work. I've been wondering if my job would consider letting me work remotely from Texas. If not, I'd need to find a job in San Antonio. I should have enough money from the trust to help me survive for awhile. Sorry for going on and on."

"That's fine . . . better than fine. I'm relieved that you're willing to move. Having you with me sounds wonderful. I was afraid you'd say that you would consider moving as a possibility. There's something else I've wanted to discuss with you. Have you thought about contacting your father? Just asking and putting it out there."

"That's a very good question. Unlike moving to Texas to be closer to you, I'm unsure about meeting my father. I want to, yet even the possibility petrifies me. I'm glad you brought it up, cuz I'm not really exactly sure how to handle the situation and want—no need—your input. Have I told you lately how glad I am that you're helping me?" Kendra said but didn't expect an answer.

"Let's talk more about that later . . . like tomorrow," Tim answered thoughtfully. "We'll give it more consideration and hopefully settle on a plan that you'll feel comfortable with. Tomorrow, I thought we could go to the office and finalize the trust. I have a notary coming in between eight o'clock and noon. I'll give her a call when we're ready. Oh, I forgot to tell you that my daddy will be in the office tomorrow and is looking forward to finally meeting you in person. I mean . . . meeting you again after thirty years or so."

Nodding her head in the affirmative, Kendra answered, "It will be nice to meet him."

"Honey, it's late and you've had a long day. You've got to be exhausted."

"You're right; I am tired. Also, I'm now aware of the Texas time difference. By golly, I've finally got it," Kendra answered.

"Let me help you up. I promise to take you back to the room and just sleep with you. No hanky-panky."

"That sounds good to me. I love snuggling with you. That doesn't mean you've already lost your desire for me . . . does it?" Kendra asked with a pouty expression on her face.

"No, that means I'm tired and full of dinner . . . as in . . . no longer hungry."

Tim walked to Kendra's side of the table. When she held out her hand and Tim helped her away from the table,

Kendra placed her head momentarily on his shoulder before saying, "Thank you for loving me and for being here for me."

While holding her closer, Tim whispered into her ear, "My pleasure . . . My Lady."

Later, as Kendra drifted off to sleep, she mumbled, "Why do you call your father "Daddy" now that you're a grown man?" She didn't hear Tim's answer—if indeed— he heard her question.

Chapter 25

Kendra woke abruptly and had a moment of not knowing where she was. Feeling silly for being a tad confused, she turned over to look at the clock. Strange, she specifically remembered Tim setting the alarm to wake them around six, and it was almost seven.

Moving away from Tim, she slowly and carefully slipped out from under the covers. Not wanting to disturb him—hearing Tim purring in his sleep—she quietly made her way to the bathroom. Even after splashing cold water on her face, she still felt wiped out and not fully awake. Keeping her eyes closed and patting the water off her face, Kendra momentarily reflected on the past . . . reminding herself of coming such a long way since stressing about every single thing . . . regardless of how trivial. If Tim only knew how awful her life used to be?

Soon after returning to Tim's side of the bed, it dawned on her that it was barely five o'clock for her. Besides, she was understandably tired from the stress of traveling and being up late. Being there for only a couple of more days, why fixate on the time difference?

Before Tim set the alarm last night, he mentioned that it would take approximately two hours to travel from San Antonio to Uvalde and hoped to be there by ten o'clock. Grimacing, she remembered her drive to that awful run-down house in Sabinal. Thank goodness, they'd by-pass that entire off-the-beaten-track area and house. Would she ever be able to put those awful visions of the holes in the floor or the disgusting smells out of her mind? Even though the house now belonged to her, hopefully it would no longer exist in her new positive world.

Right now, her decision should be about whether or not to wake Tim. While standing beside his side of the bed and while looking down at his peaceful face, she imagined how wonderful it would be to wake up every morning next to him. She leaned over and lightly patted him on the shoulder before saying, "Tim, it's after seven." With no response, she tapped a little harder and asked, "Tim, do you want to get up? It's after seven o'clock, and I think you wanted to get up around six."

Sitting up quickly and looking surprised, Tim asked, "What time is it?"

Kendra looked at the clock again before answering, "It is . . . ah, fifteen minutes after seven."

"What the hell; I set the clock for five 'til six," answered while rubbing his eyes.

"We can hurry and get out of here quickly . . . no problem . . . I'll help. Would you like me to order something to go or stop along the way for breakfast? I know breakfast is one of your favorite meals."

Walking over to check the clock, Tim answered quickly, "Good thinking. Would you mind to order us something to go? I want to jump in and take a quick shower." Still holding the clock, Tim shook his head before saying, "What a dummy I am. I set the clock for P.M.

instead of A.M. Shaking his head again, he continued, "I should have called the front desk for a wake-up call but too late now."

"We can hurry. While you shower, I'll call for breakfast and pack our stuff."

"That's why I want you with me . . . to help me," Tim said before blowing her a kiss.

On the road, Kendra helped Tim eat his breakfast burrito and take sips of orange juice and coffee in between gobbling down her own burrito and drink. "Are we having fun yet?" Tim asked.

Wiping her mouth, Kendra replied, "I always have fun with you."

"I'd be having more fun if you'd give me a kiss," Tim said before following with, "Hang on a second, so I can wipe the hot sauce off my mouth."

The traffic was heavy and stop-n-go until miles out of the city and the airport area. "Not good planning to be fighting the traffic during rush hour," Tim commented.

"This has been bad but not as awful as rush hour traffic everywhere in and around Los Angeles," Kendra interjected.

"I hear ya. I guess I should check in with the office and let them know we're on our way," Tim said.

While Tim talked first to someone named Jessica, Kendra became more interested in his conversation when he began to visit with his father. Although carefully listening, Kendra tried to appear busy cleaning up their food and drink mess . . . placing the containers and trash back into the paper sack used to carry their breakfast to the car. While concentrating on the still fairly busy traffic ahead, Kendra heard Tim say, "See you soon and thanks Daddy."

When the call was disconnected, Kendra asked, "Is everything okay."

"Everything is just fine and ready for your signatures."

"That's great. Before I forget, did I ask you something before we went to sleep last night or was I just thinking I did?"

"I'm sorry . . . but don't think so. I went right to sleep and was out until the alarm went off."

"You're kidding . . . right?" Kendra asked seriously.

"No, of course not," answered flippantly with a quizzical look on his face. "Why . . . is there a problem?" Tim inquired . . . trying to appear serious.

"Yes, if you think the alarm went off; then you definitely have a problem."

"Which is the better possibility? Would it be that I set the clock incorrectly, or convincing you that it went off but wasn't heard, or that I turned it off before the alarm sounded?" Tim asked with a grin.

"Is that what lawyers typically do?" she asked with a similar grin. "Do they tend to manipulate the outcome away from the facts?"

"Sometimes, but what you just did is similar to what a lot of my clients tend to do."

"How's that?" Kendra asked, now thoroughly confused.

"Well, they tend not to directly answer the question but answer with a question about another subject."

"Okay, you win. It's too early for me to follow all of this. My question last night—maybe asked and not heard or heard and not answered—was: Why do you still call your father . . . ah, Daddy, even though you're now an adult? I've noticed you using that expression for a long time but kept forgetting to ask why."

"Well, that will be an easy question to answer. It's kinda a Southern custom . . . Texas custom. Many children—both girls and boys—refer to their male parent as Daddy and continue to do so even as they've grown into adulthood. My friends—the ones I grew up with in Texas—still do. When I went to school in New York, I was told not to refer to my father as Daddy, because it made me appear like a country hick. So, I worked at it. However, when I first came home from New York to stay, I continued to use the word Father instead of Daddy. I'll tell you what . . . using that terminology didn't fit well with my daddy, so he sat me down and said, 'Son, I was your daddy when you were born; I was your daddy when you left home, and I'm damn sure I'll be your daddy 'til I die.' To this day, I still remember his words and our daddy/son talk. Maybe it's easy to remember because immediately after our heart-to-heart conversation, he said, 'Son, how 'bout you and your daddy go fishin'?'

"That's so interesting . . . I had no idea about that particular southern custom."

"It was just the way I was brought up. Kinda like . . . no matter what, your daddy will always have your back. Sometimes after winning a court case, he'd say to me, 'Son, your daddy ain't no dummy. He may seem like it, but sometimes it's to your advantage to let them think you're a country bumpkin.' Then, he'd laugh and laugh. My daddy was born in Alabama and came to Texas as a young boy. He graduated from college summa cum laude."

"Wow, that's very impressive," Kendra said seriously.

Giving Kendra several knowing nods, Tim offered, "Although seldom but under some rare circumstances,

I'll admit to using the term father instead of daddy." Then Tim asked, "So . . . is this a good time for us to discuss your father?"

"Yes, I think that would be a good idea. Since I'm totally conflicted on what to do, I'd really appreciate your opinion. What do you think I should do, or do you think I should do nothing?"

"How about you tell me what you've been considering doing or what you've been considering not doing. Just bounce your thoughts off me."

"Okay, here goes. Oh—and before I begin—when you're listening, you should be aware of how much I hate Clayborne. I spent many nights pacing around my apartment wondering how I could get even with him for what he did to my mother. His actions affected not only my mother, but her bitterness carried over onto me."

"Let's go over exactly what he did. Would that be okay?" Tim then asked calmly. "And do you want me to comment as you go along or wait 'til you finish?"

"Please chime in whenever you want to. To me . . . there were so many things that he did that were so terribly wrong, but then I know it's impossible for me to be objective."

Kendra began by remembering what her mother's notes divulged. "Mother wrote of feeling all alone. I think my mother was more or less held captive in that house . . . in a deserted area with no way to leave."

Tim followed with, "Was your mother abused or afraid of him, and wasn't she running away from an abusive stepfather? Didn't Clayborne let her stay to keep her safe from being found?"

"Yes, that's sorta true . . . well at first. But it was wrong of him to keep her there and keep her from going on to college . . . especially after she was eighteen."

"Are you certain that he did that? Could it have been her choice to stay? Kendra, keep in mind, I'm just asking these questions that should have been addressed by your mother. However, I do understand her situation . . . well— because of the trust—she couldn't let you know what happened for fear you'd react somehow to the situations, and she'd break one or more of the stipulations."

Becoming defensive, Kendra said, "Well, he showered her with gifts and enticed her to stay."

"Perhaps, he was only trying to make her comfortable there. I understand the place hadn't been lived in for many years. I'm just saying what Daddy passed on to me."

"Do you realize she was barely eighteen, and he was in his thirties? Not to mention, he was married and had two children."

"I'm not justifying his actions. What he did was deplorable. I'm trying to look at it from both sides. What if it started out with him doing a good deed for a young girl who needed help?"

"I don't want to look at it from both sides. What he did to my mother was one hundred per cent wrong, and there isn't another side to it."

"I'm upsetting you. Maybe I should just listen and not comment. Before we continue, do you want to ask Clayborne why he did what he did . . . like meet with him?"

"I've asked myself the same thing many times. I doubt if I could believe a single word he'd say to me. I continue to think of his terrible lies and deeds, and they'll most likely be engrained in my mind forever."

"There's a rest stop coming up in about a mile," Tim said before patting her leg and squeezing her hand. "Let's stop and leave this discussion for awhile."

As Kendra opened the restroom door, she felt certain Tim was taking Clayborne's side. Had Tim been treating her with kindness for some weird unknown reason? Why did he ask her to be with him in Texas but not ask her to marry him? Was she madly in love with Tim like her mother was with Chuck and blinded by the truth? For different reasons, she and her mother were both vulnerable when their first relationships began. How unbelievable that after all Clayborne had done to Mother—according to her mother's last apologetic letter—she wrote how she still loved Clayborne with all her heart. Thinking more about Tim's remarks, he seems to know a lot about her mother's life without reading her notes. What else did his father tell him? Maybe Tim's father was picked in order to cover-up for Clayborne, and Tim was following in his father's footsteps. Kendra began to feel sick at her stomach. Worse yet, was she on the verge of having a panic attack?

Taking slow in-and-out breaths, she started to pat her face with cold water but reminded herself not to mess up her makeup. After all, she was a changed person—both inside and out—and would never go back to being her former shy and ugly self. She'd get through this next hurdle but now needed to be extra vigilant going forward . . . with Tim and Tim's father.

Chapter 26

While Kendra remained quiet on the remaining stretch to Uvalde, Tim talked about living in Texas, the passing scenery, and current events. He knew Kendra was upset when he'd earlier played devil's advocate to her remarks about Clayborne. Although merely expressing opposing possibilities—like on a debate team—he soon realized that Kendra was too personally involved to be part of a back-and-forth discussion about Clayborne. He'd assumed their relationship had progressed to the point of discussing anything . . . even Clayborne, but that notion quickly showed itself to be incorrect. She had noticeably jumped from the start of her mother's relationship with Clayborne to the time of deceit. Nowhere close to what he was trying to convey or accomplish, he was now certain that his questions and offering possibilities were received as a direct affront to Kendra's way of thinking or what she believed. Now aware that Kendra wasn't in a good place emotionally, his daddy was sure right when he cautioned him to go easy on her.

Naturally, he had no idea of what actually happened during Kendra's mother's time in Texas, but also couldn't keep from wondering if Kendra knew the whole truth or just thought she did. Perhaps Kendra's mother was aware of Clayborne being married and decided to stay with him anyway. Whatever the circumstances, he knew Kendra was hurting, and he needed to somehow come up with a way to help her. So for now, he'd take off his lawyer hat, take off his debate team hat, and take off his objective hat and concentrate on repairing the obvious distance between them. Realizing it was a sensitive subject for Kendra to address, perhaps it would be better for her to discuss whether or not to meet with Clayborne with his daddy. After all, his daddy had a better insight into her mother's past with Clayborne and possibly into Kendra's past. Lost in his thoughts, he definitely needed to assure Kendra that he was only trying to help her.

To that end, Tim turned down the radio before saying, "Kendra, I know that you're upset with me, but I honestly meant no harm."

When he received no response, Tim continued, "If I said anything to offend you, I'm sincerely sorry. Would you like to discuss your mother's relationship with Clayborne with my daddy?"

"Maybe, but I have my mother's notes to go by. Nothing anyone can say to me—not you or your father— will change anything that I've read . . . and in my mother's own handwriting."

Wanting to veer away from Kendra's frosty—even combative—attitude, he rather bluntly said, "I'm not the enemy here. I remember you saying . . . something about your therapist said it was important to work together. Can we go back to doing that?"

"Maybe, but I only wanted your opinion on whether to meet with Clayborne or not."

"I understand that, but remember . . . I was just chiming in. You said that would be okay."

Without giving Kendra time to respond, Tim added, "Perhaps I got into the mode of prepping a client for trial or giving insight into subjects that might come up during a discussion . . . if indeed the discussion happened. Kendra, I'm on your side and here to assist you. Are you even listening to what I'm saying?"

Without looking in Tim's direction, she thoughtfully and quietly answered, "I am listening, but I'm also dealing with what's the truth and what isn't. While Mother lived year in and year out—consumed by bitterness—the truth was purposely hidden from me. In turn and being totally honest . . . well, because of the way she raised me; it's difficult for me to judge people. Since you've lived a normal life while growing up with the perfect family and father, I'm sure you have no idea what I'm even talking about. I—on the other hand—have a difficult time with many things in many areas."

"Am I one of those areas?" Tim asked solemnly.

"I'm not sure now. I didn't think so, but you did take Clayborne's side."

"Is it possible that you misunderstood my words or me?" Tim inquired.

Pausing and receiving no reply, Tim continued in a quiet yet direct manner. "Maybe I've been wrong about our feelings for each other. I thought we loved each other, and that was all that mattered. Am I wrong?"

Pausing again to wait for a reply, Tim offered, "I guess when you're not answering, I'll assume I've been wrong. Going forward, we should keep all discussions on a businesslike level. Better yet, it's my opinion that my daddy should handle everything for you going forward."

While remaining silent and preferring not to give Tim an answer, Kendra realized they were entering the town of Uvalde. Purposely changing the subject, she asked, "Are we close to your office?"

"Yes, a few blocks away. Kendra, you didn't give me an answer on talking to my daddy about meeting Clayborne or not? In fact, you've given me very few answers about anything."

"I think I'll play it by ear," she replied flippantly. "It depends on how I feel when the paperwork is finished. Then, I'll decide."

Parking in front of the office, Tim noticed Kendra's attitude had changed from being a sensitive and personable individual into someone he didn't recognize. Frowning, he asked himself what the hell had just happened, and what the hell was wrong with her? Doing his best to be objective, he was certain he'd said nothing wrong and was pissed.

As Tim stopped the car, Kendra reminded herself that she was there to make her own choices . . . not anyone else's. Without his usual smile, Kendra watched Tim walk around the car and open her door. His disposition was different and more like a parking attendant's demeanor.

Chapter 27

Usually when helping Kendra from the car, Tim would lean inward and kiss her whenever their faces were close. But even if he'd wanted to—which he didn't at the moment—Kendra had already turned her head away . . . most likely on purpose, so the kiss would have landed on her cheek or forehead anyway. Recollections of his previous marriage suddenly crossed his mind.

Stepping out of the car, Kendra had gone from feeling confident and excited about meeting John Blevins to wanting to hide from him. In spite of her feelings for Tim—which she was now questioning—could she trust what his father would tell her? Also, she was again wondering whether Clayborne and John Blevins had communicated about her through the years. So, regardless of what John Blevins would tell her, she'd take as long as necessary to read each and every word of the papers she'd be signing. And, she was determined not to be pressured into signing anything that wasn't one hundred per cent in her best interest; deciding to address this situation in the same manner as she'd dealt with her new job position. If she didn't like what was being presented to her, she'd simply walk away. Thank goodness she wasn't in her mother's position years ago . . . forced to leave Texas with nothing but an unwanted child.

Stepping onto the sidewalk, Kendra took a moment to glance at the front of the law office. It wasn't anything like the ones she'd seen in Los Angeles . . . located in tall buildings with large lobbies and elevators. The building in front of her was a one story with narrow stores arranged in a row . . . separated by different yet similar store fronts and advertisements.

Once inside, the room reminded her of an intake sitting area of a postal annex . . . small with a counter in the middle, separating access to the back area on both sides.

A young lady with a friendly smile immediately pushed back from a desk behind the counter and walked hurriedly to the opening beside the counter. "Welcome back, Mr. Blevins. Your daddy is waiting for you in his office."

"Thank you, Jessica. I'd like to introduce you to Kendra Smith . . . a longtime client of ours."

After a short introduction and Jessica saying, "Hello and welcome," Tim asked, "Is the notary waiting for us or do you need to give her a call?"

"Yes, the notary is here and in the conference room. Are you ready for her?"

"No, we'll say hello to John first," Tim answered in a businesslike manner.

While addressing both of them, Jessica asked, "Can I get y'all something to drink?" Before either replied, she added, "My bosses like the fridge stocked with drinks and there's hot coffee."

Looking at Kendra and seeing her head shake in a negative direction, Tim replied, "I guess we're good.

While I take Miss Smith back, would you inform the notary that we're here, and she'll be needed in a few minutes?"

Approaching John Blevins's office, Kendra could feel her heart pounding. She thought about reaching out and taking Tim's hand—nowadays, an almost natural habit—but reconsidered and didn't. When they entered his open door, John immediately saw them and rushed over to greet them . . . surprising Kendra with a bear hug. Even before saying anything, he pushed her back to arm's length before grinning and uttering, "Hi little darlin'! I'm so happy to finally meet you face-to-face. Has my son been obliging while minding his P's and Q's?"

"Yes, I guess so," Kendra replied without enthusiasm . . . wondering what in the world he was talking about . . . not understanding what P's and Q's meant.

"Are you thirsty . . . hungry? Anything I can get for you before we begin."

"I'm fine . . . thank you. I just want to finally get this over with," Kendra responded.

"I bet you do. Bless your heart. Where would you feel the most comfortable . . . in the conference room, here in my office, or Tim's office?" he inquired with a smile.

"Where would be the best place for me to sit and quietly read what I'll be signing?"

"I'm thinking the conference room would be best. There would be no people or phone interruptions and more room on the table for the notary to spread out the papers."

When John said, "Follow me," Tim interjected, "I'll be there later. I need to check my messages to see if something important needs my immediate attention."

Seemingly perplexed, John replied rather sternly, "Nothin' is more important than taking care of Kendra. She's been waiting too long as it is."

As if Tim didn't hear his daddy's words—more like flatly ignoring them—he abruptly turned toward an open door on the opposite side of the short hallway and disappeared. Although obviously confused, John Blevins continued to lead Kendra toward a doorway at the end of the hallway marked Conference Room.

Opening the door before stepping aside—so Kendra could enter before him—John introduced her to the notary. "Where would you like me to sit?" Kendra asked.

Pulling a chair away from the large table, John answered, "How about here. I'll sit beside you and answer any of the questions you may have. You should never sign anything until you feel confident that you fully understand what you're signing. I know you and Tim have become close, would you like me to fetch him before we begin?"

"No . . . but thank you for asking. I'm sure you'll be able to answer any of my questions. After all, you've been dealing with this through the years and helped my mother from the beginning of setting up the trust."

Still baffled by the obvious coolness between the two of them, John wanted to ask if there was a problem but decided to wait until the papers were signed and the business part of the meeting was completed. Besides, it didn't seem right to discuss personal matters in front of the notary. After a slight pause to get settled, John said, "Okay, let's begin with the trust itself. I know you've read it, but

I've recently gone back through it and have a few clips on sections that I want to make sure you understand."

Kendra was more than pleasantly surprised by how organized the paperwork had been laid out on the conference table. As she glanced over the different items, she thought how she'd done them the same way before entering them into a database. Taking her time and not concerned that John Blevins and the notary were waiting, she carefully flipped over each page. While nothing stood out from what she already knew or expected, she kept waiting for something wrong to show itself. If her therapist was here, she would have told her she was practicing negative thinking, but at the moment she didn't care.

There was a detailed recap of the trust's bank account. She was surprised that the bank balance was a little more than she'd originally been told. There was a new signature card attached for transferring the balance into an account with only her name. But even more surprising . . . there were no deductions for services from the law firm during the last year except for this present meeting expenses . . . such as notary service, filing charges due the court for recording fees, and having the house deed transferred into her name. The lack of charges meant that Tim had used his own money to visit her, paying for his own transportation, hotel expenses, meals, and etcetera. She started to ask John Blevins about Tim's lack of fees and charges but decided now wasn't the time, noting it was none of the notary's business.

While listening to John Blevins tell the notary to give the paperwork to Jessica out front, thanking her for her service, and wishing her a nice day, Kendra asked herself what she should do now that everything was finished. After weighing some possible options but before coming to a decision, John suggested, "C'mon, let's go back to my office and sit a spell."

Feeling somewhat uneasy, Kendra followed him back to his office. Purposely looking ahead to the door Tim entered earlier; it was now closed. Arriving at John's office, he stepped aside so she could enter first. When she cautiously walked inside, John quickly moved around her . . . assisting her into a chair directly in front of his desk. Beginning to feel oddly relaxed, she thought . . . now I know where Tim gets his nice manners. Barely seated behind his desk, John inquired, "So . . . what's with the cool temperature between the two of you? What's going on?"

"It's all too embarrassing to talk about," Kendra answered with her head down.

"Not with me . . . Honey. Even though you weren't aware of me, I was probably the closest person to you while you were growing up. I'm thinking you're in your early thirties 'bout now, and that's a long time. I've watched you grow from childhood to adulthood but only from the outer edges. Taking care of your expenses helped me follow your activities through the years. While neither your mother nor I could explain anything to you, I've been aware of the difficult times you've encountered. Your mother periodically discussed with me the best ways to handle different situations, and I willingly offered my opinions. I did as much as I could to assist her but never actually knew if she followed any of my suggestions or how the end results affected you . . . other than financially. If you'll look carefully through the recap sheets, you'll get a pretty good view of your life." Pausing a moment to let his words settle in, he added, "Jessica has copies of everything you signed today and additionally . . . ah, your complete file. I don't want anything hidden from you anymore."

"I sure appreciate that, and yes, I already noticed the recap sheets. It was like going back through memory lane. Do you mind to answer a few questions for me? I need help with answers that I can't obtain from anyone else? I'm hoping you'll be able to fill in some of the behind the scenes information . . . ah, answers that I've been unable to learn from Mother's notes."

"Of course . . . but keep in mind that I was probably more hands on because Clayborne didn't want to be kept in the loop. He insisted that he didn't want to know anything . . . opting out of receiving any personal or financial updates regarding the trust. However, and even though I didn't forward the information to him—as per his written instructions—I have continued to keep the records for safekeeping. One can never know . . . perhaps for my own protection."

"Please understand that I don't mean to bombard you with questions, but I really want to put all of this behind me. Thank you for your help today and through the years. I had no idea."

"How about this idea, and keep in mind I don't want to interfere with your plans, but would you and Tim like to join me for dinner . . . sorta a celebration dinner?"

"As far as I know, no plans have been made. I was trying to decide what I should do . . . like getting back to the airport to fly home. I'm thinking it's too late now to make plans for that to happen today, so I'll need to find a hotel. I'd really like to talk more over dinner. I really can't speak for what Tim's plans are."

"I'll find out what he's planning for tonight. He's been real excited about you being here. Remember . . . there is nothing you can ask me or want to know that would be too embarrassing to discuss. You are like my long lost daughter coming home. I think of you as family, so we can openly visit about anything now."

"I don't know what to say. I've never felt like part of a family before," she replied introspectively. "Mother didn't want me around, made me feel like I didn't exist, so I always felt alone and unwanted."

"Let me tell you something . . . little lady. The family you come from isn't as important as the family who wants you. And, as ole Conway Twitty sang in his song "Help Me Make It Through the Night," 'Yesterday is done and gone, and tomorrow's out of sight.' That's so true; don't you reckon? Then, the words I'd say were the most important ones, 'And it's sad to be alone.' Honey, that's the truth; I'll attest to that. Being alone is the pits."

"I understand what you're saying. Been there . . . done that," Kendra answered and smiled.

"Well, how 'bout we finish up for now? Before we fetch Tim, I'm still not sure what going on with you two, but Tim's had a hankerin' for you for as long as he's known you. Frankly, he's not been this interested in anyone since his divorce. I'm not saying he hasn't had lots of lady friends now and then but nothing on a permanent basis. He's the one who insisted on getting involved in handling the trust, traveling to California, and the likes."

Kendra blurted out, "I'm angry with him for taking Clayborne's side when I only asked his opinion on whether or not I should meet with Clayborne."

"Whoa . . . now; I'm not taking sides but—to use your terminology—Tim is totally on your side and committed to helping you. That's the honest to God's truth and a fact I'd base my life on . . . no ifs, ands, or buts about it," John replied firmly yet kindly.

"I'm so messed up . . . damaged even. Maybe there's no hope for me, and I'm beyond repair. I have such terrible trust issues."

"Honey, you've got gumption. I can attest to that after your last hospital stay."

Taking a quick moment to grasp his remark, Kendra was not only caught off guard but found herself momentarily embarrassed and speechless. While also feeling somewhat defensive; at least his remark eliminated one of the questions she'd previously debated about asking. So . . . he knew.

"So, you know about that?" she asked cautiously.

"Yes ma'am. As the legal backup on the trust, my contact information was on all of yours and your mother's medical and insurance forms. I'm thinking you already noticed that. Anyway, because of your mother's accident and passing during your problem time, I asked to be informed about your condition on a daily basis. During that same time, I was also dealing with your mother's house and the rest of it. Well, you know."

"I had no idea. That entire time is such a blur to me. I saw in the trust that Mother said she wanted to be cremated, but I never knew what happened with her ashes."

Without addressing Kendra's last remark, John said, "Darlin', I've got a meeting coming up in about thirty minutes. I surely want to answer all your questions and give you closure going forward but don't want to rush through it. Let's continue this at dinner."

"Okay, but I need to ask you one quick question."

"Go ahead and then we'll get Tim and pick up your papers from the front office."

Before asking, Kendra swallowed and cleared her throat. "Does Tim know about my episode, and why I was in the hospital?"

"Not from me . . . absolutely not! That would be your choice to tell him or not."

Chapter 28

During the short walk to Tim's office, Kendra couldn't keep from wondering how she'd be received by Tim. She was also reflecting on his father's last remark of, "Your choice to tell him or not." Watching John Blevins tap on Tim's door and enter before receiving a response, she was still undecided. However, when she saw Tim's indifferent face, she knew there were several new decisions to be made . . . some more important than others . . . some sooner than later.

Tim seemed amendable to going to dinner, even offering to drive Kendra to the hotel and wait until she was registered. He was polite and helpful but didn't go out-of-his-way to be extra attentive like in the past. She was polite in return but missed the closeness they'd once shared.

After helping take her luggage to the room, Tim asked, "Would you like me to pick you up for dinner . . . say about 6:30?"

"That would be nice," she answered . . . just as politely.

"Okay, you have my cell number in case you change your mind."

Watching Tim turn to leave, Kendra offered, "In case you're interested; I've decided not to meet with Clayborne." Waiting for a reply and receiving none, she added, "He wanted nothing to do with me, so I want nothing to do with him." Then added off-handedly, "What's the point?"

Craving some sort of feedback about her decision, she waited again for Tim to respond. As Kendra watched him walk toward the door and then pause, she was both surprised and dismayed by his reply of "Whatever."

When the door closed behind him, Kendra began to cry. She knew she'd messed up . . . big time. Tim didn't want her any more, her mother never wanted her, and now she'd go back to being alone. Conway Twitty's words were right, 'And it's sad to be alone.' For the first time in months, she took a tranquilizer, flopped down on the bed, and began to cry.

* * *

As John Blevins helped with her chair at dinner, Kendra couldn't believe how much her relationship with Tim had changed in such a short period of time. Even dressing for dinner felt different . . . almost unimportant. Usually, she'd worry about whether Tim would like her outfit or perfume . . . fixating on each item she put on from top to bottom. Only a week had passed since her latest shopping spree to buy sexy underwear and sleep garments. Basically, her entire world had been planned around being with him. After studying the expense sheets and learning that no charges had been submitted by Tim—not for his help or for anything he'd done or spent—she had definitely misjudged him by instinctively questioning his motives.

Knowing it wasn't wise to mix tranquilizers with alcohol, Kendra declined to have a drink before ordering dinner. However, both John and Tim ordered their favorite beers.

When John asked if she was a teetotaler, she answered, "Nothing sounds good to me, so I'll just have a cup of hot tea."

Having remained quiet while seeming to concentrate on his menu and settle on what to order, Tim asked . . . bordering on sarcastically, "Doesn't even a screwdriver sound good?"

"No, I'll stick with the tea . . . but thank you," Kendra answered matter-of-factly.

Looking at Tim, his daddy said, "That'll work. I was thinkin' we should order Champagne to celebrate the ending of the trust and Kendra moving on with her life, but we can toast with tea and beer just the same. What do you think . . . Son?"

"Whatever you want to do sounds fine with me. I'm also glad it's ending and over with."

"Okay . . . what's going on with y'all? Let's talk about it and get it out in the open. I think it's way past time for me to understand or at least hear what's going on with you two. Please tell me so we can talk about it . . . like a family should do."

Knowing John was more of a "more direct person" than either of them seemed to be, Kendra wanted to put the inevitable talk out of the way . . . perhaps until after the meal—or perhaps not at all—so asked, "Could we order our meal first? I'm really hungry. We or I haven't eaten since having breakfast burritos early this morning."

"Sure thing, Honey. I had no idea." Turning toward Tim, he said, "You should have said something about this little lady being hungry. We could have put on the feed bag sooner."

"I'm not a mind reader . . . ah, stomach reader," Tim answered in an odd way.

Kendra couldn't look in Tim's direction. First of all, she wasn't being truthful about being hungry and secondly, they had both agreed not to stop for lunch since they were running late.

Looking in Kendra's direction, John said in an upbeat way, "You know when Timothy's momma, Annabelle, was in the family way with Tim, she quit drinking alcohol and drank tea. Is there somethin' else we should be celebrating?"

Immediately understanding his query, Kendra answered convincingly, "No . . . for sure not."

"Too bad cuz I can't think of anything better than retiring and taking a grandchild fishin'."

"I understand what you are saying, but I can't think of anything worse than being pregnant, unmarried, and alone like my mother was."

When the table became quiet, Kendra felt relieved to move away from that uncomfortable and horrible scenario. She somewhat relaxed when Tim waved to the waiter to come to their table and take their food orders. Tim also ordered another beer for himself and his daddy."

"Could we toast now?" John asked before raising his glass.

"Here's to Kendra signing the trust and moving away from her past problems and moving on to a happy future."

As they clicked the two beer glasses and cup together, Tim said, "I'll drink to that."

Kendra followed with, "Wouldn't that be wonderful?"

Just as the toast was completed, the waiter arrived with two fresh beers, more hot water, and another tea bag for Kendra.

"While we wait for our vittles, who wants to tell me what's going on?" Looking from side-to-side at each of them, John felt like an arbitrator—or a neutral third party—trying to get to the bottom of a dispute. "Have the two of you figured out that I'm not going to stop askin'? So, let's get at it. There's definitely a problem here that needs to be aired out. If neither of you don't want to discuss it, then . . . damn it, say so."

When silence surrounded the table again, John said, "So be it. Now, if I can remember, I'm going to talk about the questions Kendra brought up earlier that weren't addressed. Let me see." Looking directly at Kendra, he continued, "You wanted to know about your momma's ashes. Well, she sent me a personal note with lots of directions . . . saying that I could help her or not, and tell her daughter or not. She also told me not to worry, cuz she'd never know if I did or didn't follow through with her wishes. She asked if I'd scatter her ashes by the rose bushes in front of the Sabinal house. Now . . . mind you, those rose bushes were a few dried-up stumps when I went out there. Regardless of the awful drive, I wanted to do as your mamma asked me to do." Staring off for a moment, John finally continued, "Oh, how that woman loved that house. It wasn't much when she was there, but she felt like it was hers. Kendra, I know how you think of the house as being disgusting . . . and it is, but your momma was happy there. I'm thinking it was—most likely—the last time she was ever happy."

"What else did she ask you to do?" Kendra asked . . . truly interested.

"Well, let me think on it. She asked me to move any of the personal items from the living area to the attic, and to be sure to lock the attic door."

"Did that include the trunk?"

"Even though I had already assured her that Chuck would never go there again, the short answer is yes . . . I moved the trunk into the attic."

"How could you be so certain?" Kendra asked.

"That wasn't difficult, cuz he was so paranoid that his family would find out what he'd done."

"Are you talking about his immediate family or his whole family?" Kendra questioned.

Both . . . he was very ashamed of what he'd done. He begged your momma not to let his wife know that he'd been living a double life . . . much less that your mamma was expecting his child."

"Wait a minute. Are you saying my mother knew he was married?"

"Yes, she absolutely did. She not only knew but demanded that he divorce his wife and marry her."

"Did he tell you that or did my mother tell you that?" Kendra asked in a direct manner.

"Both told me. He loved your mother very much but not enough to give up everything for her. Remember . . . he already had two little boys and the beginnings of a cattle empire."

"So, you think that was okay?"

"Kendra, I'm not making any judgments here. I'm just trying to inform you about the facts of what happened back then. I'm just the messenger here."

"Sorry, I have so much hate for him, and what he did to my mother . . . and eventually to me. His actions and lies were incomprehensible, and it's difficult for me to dismiss them or him."

"I understand that you're stuck in a hate mode. But you should understand that I'm here to help you—as I'm sure Tim is—so what would you like me or Tim to do? Since you've decided not to meet with Clayborne, what are your wishes regarding him going forward?"

"I've thought about somehow hurting his campaign. I've thought about somehow hurting his immediate family. I've even thought about somehow hurting his family's empire. Right now, I'm still undecided on what I want or how I want to proceed."

"We can initiate any of what you just mentioned, but I'm hard-pressed—at this point in time—how any of it will actually help you or your mother?" John answered sincerely. "While keeping in mind the hurt you could be creating to some of his family, do you think the end result will actually make you feel better or make your life better? He's divorced and his children are adults now. I'm also thinking that politically, he'll just say that any of these wild accusations are manufactured by his opponent without facts, or something along those lines."

"Sounds like you're taking sides like Tim," Kendra answered somberly.

Before John could reply, their food arrived, and Kendra hoped the subject was closed.

After the waiter left, John said, "Remember, you have choices, and we are here to help. It is totally up to you on how you want to proceed."

"I guess since everything is now settled with the trust, I have time to think about it."

"Please keep in mind that I did everything within my power to help your mother throughout the years. Maybe you'd feel better if you did meet Claiborne face-to-face. Maybe you'd feel worse. Whatever you decide, we'll be here to assist you with the particulars . . . like place and time. Or, maybe you'd rather contact another law firm without our assistance. Again, it's up to you . . . your choice."

Answering quickly, Kendra said, "Right now, I just want to go home. I'm not only angry with Clayborne, but I'm also angry with my mother for so many reasons . . . especially now that I've learned that she knew he was married and still stayed with him. Do you know if she found out he was married before or after she got pregnant with me?"

"Sorry Hon . . . I can't help you there." John answered honestly but kindly.

Barely picking at her meal, all Kendra wanted to do was leave. While eating, everyone became quiet with little conversation around the table. After John asked for the bill, he offered, "After I sign for our dinner, I'm going to leave y'all alone to talk."

Pushing slowly away from the table, John stood, smiled, and rubbed his stomach. Hesitating and seemingly lost in thought, he leaned over and kissed Kendra on the cheek, before saying, "Have a safe trip home and don't hesitate to call me." Seemingly far away in thought again, he added, "Honey, I know full well the hell you've been through during your lifetime, but nothin' can ever change the past. I'm thinkin' . . . it's best to let it go . . . like your mother's ashes. In spite of your life leading up 'til now, I think you should concentrate on finding a future full of love and happiness. Those are just the fatherly words I'd say to my daughter. Take it from an old man, some things can't be fixed. Best to deal with it, and like I said before . . . let it go."

Beginning to tear up, Kendra responded, "Thank you for helping Mother through the years and for helping me." As she watched John leave, Kendra wondered if she'd ever see him again.

After an uncomfortable silence, Tim said, "I hate that we have this distance between us. Can we talk?" When Kendra didn't reply and continued to keep her head down, Tim said, "I've told you numerous times how much I love you—even from the very beginning—but for some reason you've shut me out and held my words against me because of Clayborne. I don't think you'd done that if you felt the same way about me . . . ah, as I feel about you."

Kendra slowly lifted her head but didn't respond. Without a reply, Tim resumed, "Having said that; I guess I'll be upfront with you and tell you exactly what my plans were after you finished signing the trust papers. I had been very careful and going out of my way to separate my feelings from anything to do with the trust or with my father setting up the trust. While keeping that in mind, I was planning to ask you to marry me. I had also asked one of my best friends and a long time client—who owns a data processing business in San Antonio—if he would be interested in interviewing you for a position in his company. He told me that my recommendation was enough for him . . . adding that he was excited that I was moving the practice to San Antonio and couldn't wait to play one-on-one with me again. After saying all this, I don't think we're on the same page any more about having a future together. I think—and maybe because of your mother—you're not ready to be with me or perhaps anyone."

"Perhaps you're right," Kendra answered. "Maybe I need more time to understand what love is really about. I do love you, but my mother loved Clayborne too while she despised me . . . treating me with total disgust. I'm so mixed up, and you deserve someone much better than me."

Shaking his head and confused over Kendra's reply, Tim asked, "Are you ready to go back to the hotel?"

"Yes, I think so."

"I heard you tell Daddy that you made a reservation to fly back to California tomorrow."

"Yes, I did," Kendra answered somewhat defensively.

"Would you like me to drive you to the airport?" Tim asked sincerely.

"No, I've already made plans for a car to pick me up . . . but thanks."

"Kendra . . . remember, I'll be here if you ever want to talk. And, I hope you'll consider my suggestions of moving to San Antonio and checking out the job possibility. It could be a new start for you. Above anything else, I'd be happy if our relationship could get back on track sometime in the future." With no answer to Tim's comments, their conversation concluded.

The short trip back to the hotel was awkward and quiet. Tim felt he'd put his cards on the table, and Kendra was deep in thought, contemplating what she might do after hurting Tim.

When they arrived back at the hotel, Tim parked in front of the hotel entrance, obviously not planning to park in the hotel's parking lot or go in. They impersonally hugged each other and said their somewhat ill at ease goodbyes. Tim's last words were, Kendra, "I'll always love you," and Kendra's final reply, "I'll always love you too."

Epilogue

Five Years Later

"Tim, when you finish packing the fishing stuff, would you mind to help Timmy get into his car seat? I hoped I've gathered everything important for the baby into the diaper bag, but I've probably forgotten something. Your poor father, he's probably been pacing the floor for hours while waiting for us."

"Is Annie awake yet?" Tim asked.

"Not yet. I've been waiting until the last minute to wake her."

Tim walked up behind Kendra and kissed her on the back of the neck before whispering, "Are you as happy with our life as I am?"

While turning around to kiss him, Kendra answered, "More, and as I often tell your father . . . ah, our Daddy, you're the greatest choice I've ever made."

Made in the USA
Las Vegas, NV
06 May 2025

21799988R00203